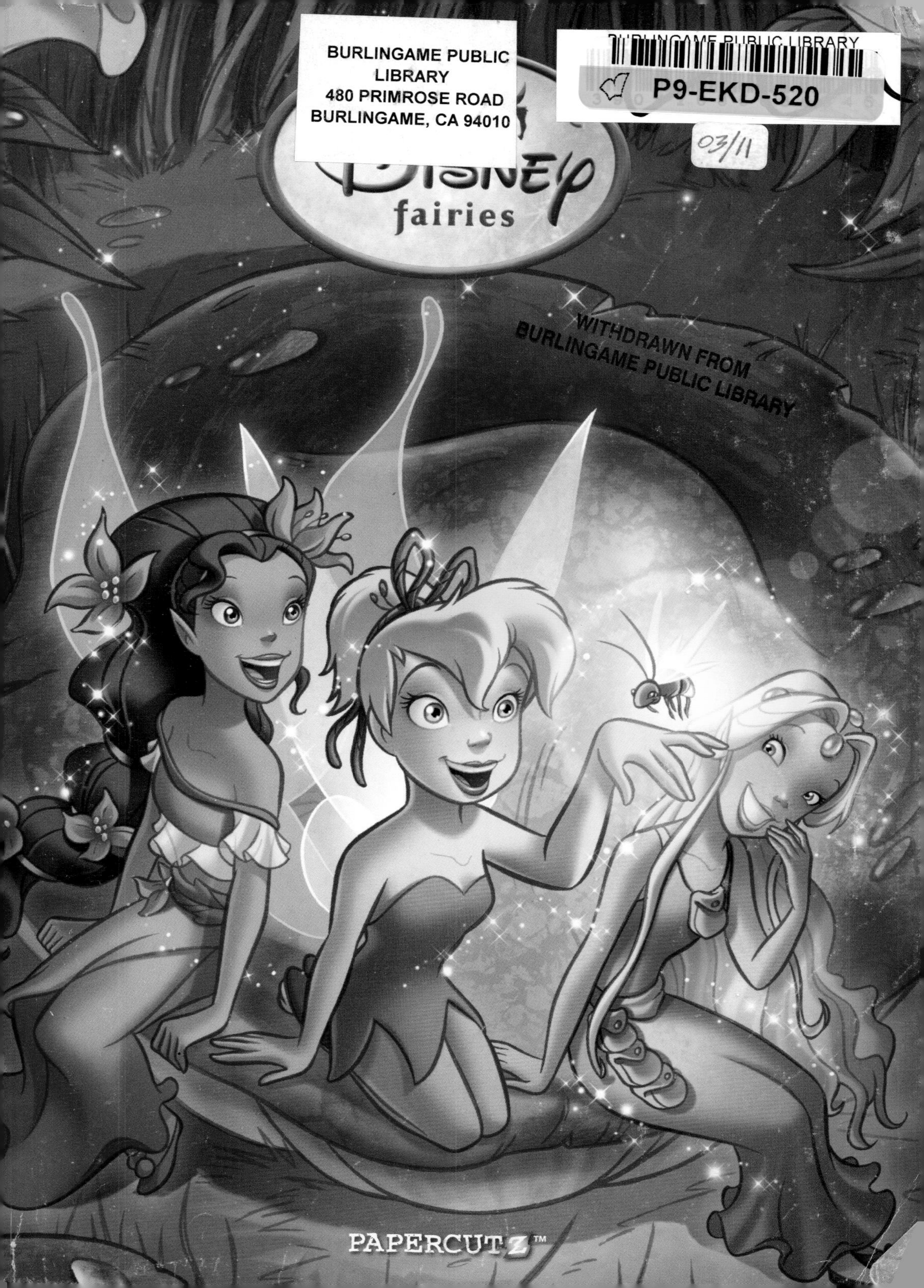
Disney
fairies
PAPERCUTZ™

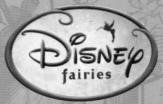

Disney fairies

Graphic Novels Available from PAPERCUTZ

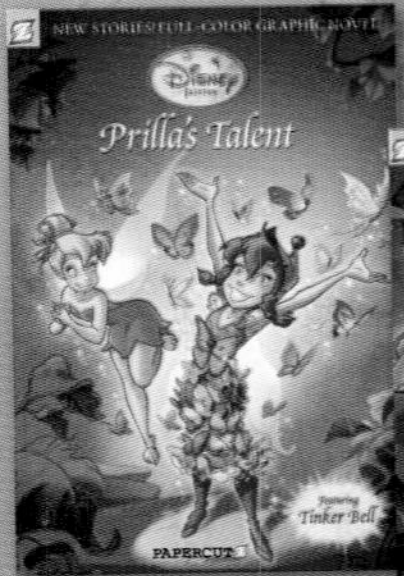
NEW STORIES! FULL-COLOR GRAPHIC NOVEL
Disney fairies
Prilla's Talent
PAPERCUTZ

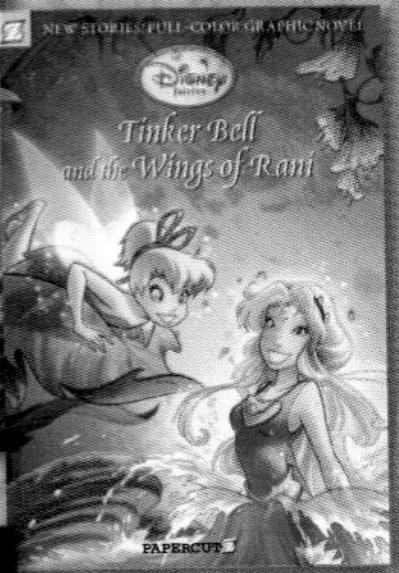
NEW STORIES! FULL-COLOR GRAPHIC NOVEL
Disney fairies
Tinker Bell and the Wings of Rani
PAPERCUTZ

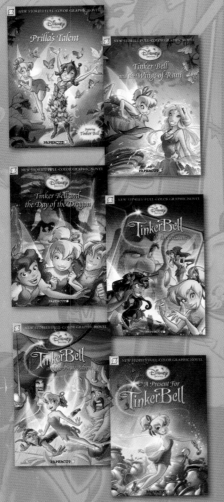

Graphic Novel #1
"Prilla's Talent"

Graphic Novel #2
"Tinker Bell and the Wings of Rani"

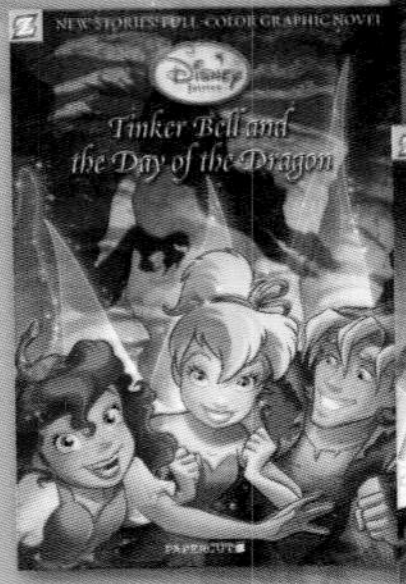
NEW STORIES! FULL-COLOR GRAPHIC NOVEL
Disney fairies
Tinker Bell and the Day of the Dragon
PAPERCUTZ

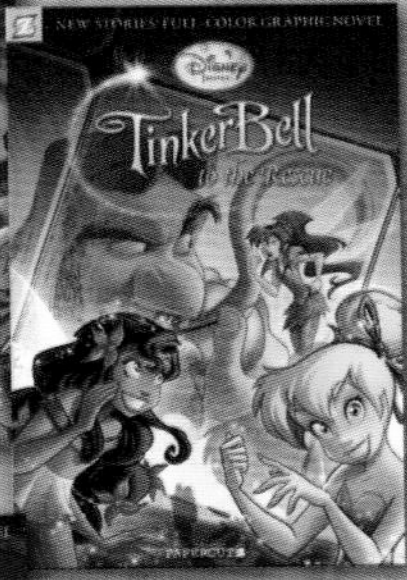
NEW STORIES! FULL-COLOR GRAPHIC NOVEL
Disney fairies
TinkerBell
PAPERCUTZ

Graphic Novel #3
"Tinker Bell and the Day of the Dragon"

Graphic Novel #4
"Tinker Bell to the Rescue"

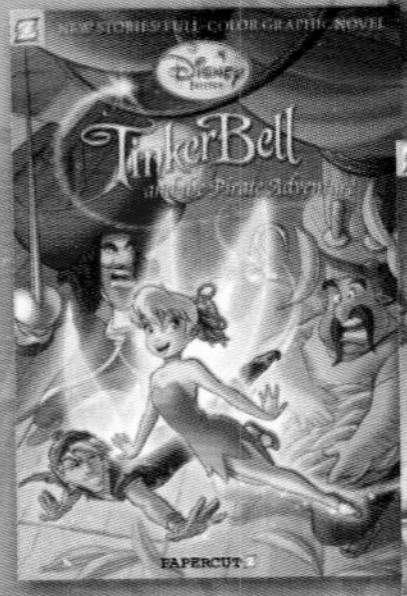
NEW STORIES! FULL-COLOR GRAPHIC NOVEL
Disney fairies
TinkerBell
PAPERCUTZ

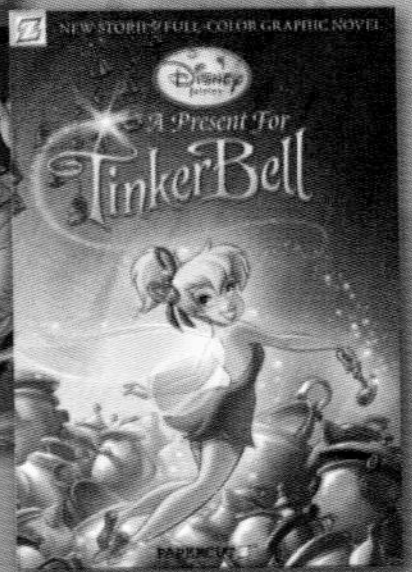
NEW STORIES! FULL-COLOR GRAPHIC NOVEL
Disney fairies
A Present For TinkerBell
PAPERCUTZ

Graphic Novel #5
"Tinker Bell and the Pirate Adventure"

Coming Soon:
Graphic Novel #6
"A Present for Tinker Bell"

Disney Fairies graphic novels are available in paperback for $7.99 each; in hardcover for $12.99 each except #5 and 6, $6.99PB, $10.99HC. Available through all booksellers.

See more at www.papercutz.com

Or you can order through us: please add $4.00 for postage and handling for the first book, and add $1.00 for each additional book. Please make check payable to NBM Publishing. Send to: Papercutz, 1200 County Rd., Rte 523, Flemington, NJ 08222 or call 800 886 1223 (9-6 EST M-F) MC-Visa-Amex accepted

#5 "Tinker Bell and the Pirate Adventure"

Contents

Wings of Fire   5

The Pirates Go Bananas   18

Beck's Beautiful Surprise   31

When the Little Lights Went Out   44

PAPERCUTZ™

NEW YORK

"Wings of Fire"
Script: Paola Mulazzi
Revised Dialogue: Cortney Faye Powell
Pencils: Elisabetta Melaranci
Inks: Marina Baggio and Cristina Giorgilli
Color: Stefania Santi
Page 5 Art:
Pencils: Andrea Greppi
Inks: Roberta Zanotta
Color: Andrea Cagol

"Beck's Beautiful Surprise"
Script: Silvia Giannatti
Revised Dialogue: Cortney Faye Powell
Pencils: Elisabetta Melaranci
Inks: Cristina Giorgilli
Color: Stefania Santi
Page 31 Art:
Pencils: Gianluca Barone
Inks: Roberta Zanotta
Color: Andrea Cagol

"The Pirates Go Bananas"
Script: Augusto Macchetto
Revised Dialogue: Cortney Faye Powell
Pencils: Andrea Greppi
Inks: Roberta Zanotta
Color: Stefania Santi
Page 18 Art:
Pencils: Andrea Greppi
Inks: Marina Baggio
Color: Andrea Cagol

"When the Little Lights Went Out"
Script: Paola Mulazzi
Revised Dialogue: Cortney Faye Powell
Pencils: Emilio Urbano and Manuela Razzi
Inks: Roberta Zanotta
Color: Stefania Santi
Page 44 Art:
Pencils: Andrea Greppi
Inks: Marina Baggio
Colors: Andrea Cagol

Chris Nelson and Caitlin Hinrichs – Production
Special Thanks – Jesse Post and Shiho Tilley
Michael Petranek – Associate Editor
Jim Salicrup – Editor-in-Chief

ISBN: 978-1-59707-240-3 paperback edition
ISBN: 978-1-59707-241-0 hardcover edition

Printed in Singapore. December 2010
by Tien Wah Press PTE LTD
4 Pandan Crescent
Singapore 128475

Distributed by Macmillan.

First Printing

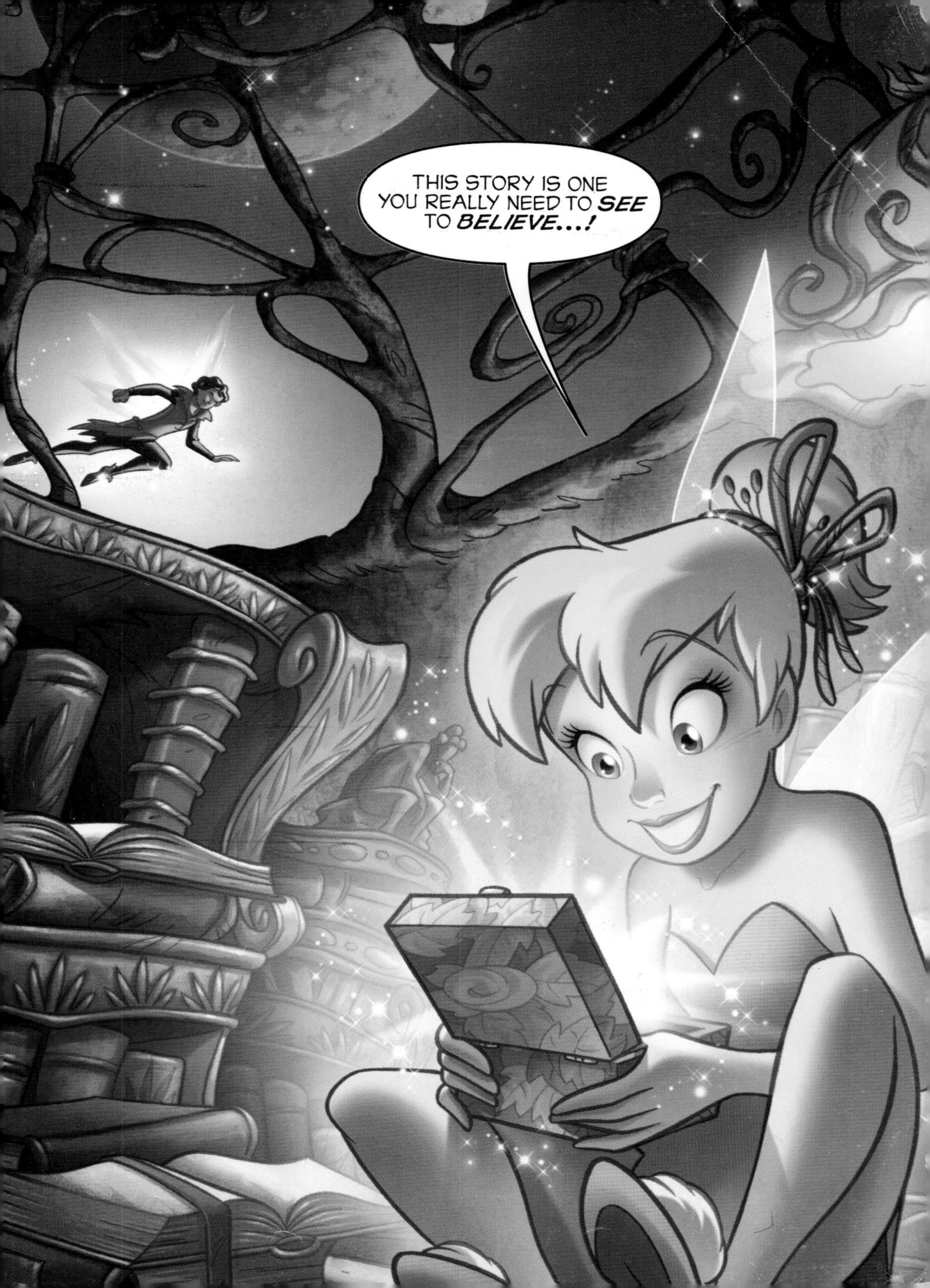
THIS STORY IS ONE YOU REALLY NEED TO SEE TO BELIEVE...!

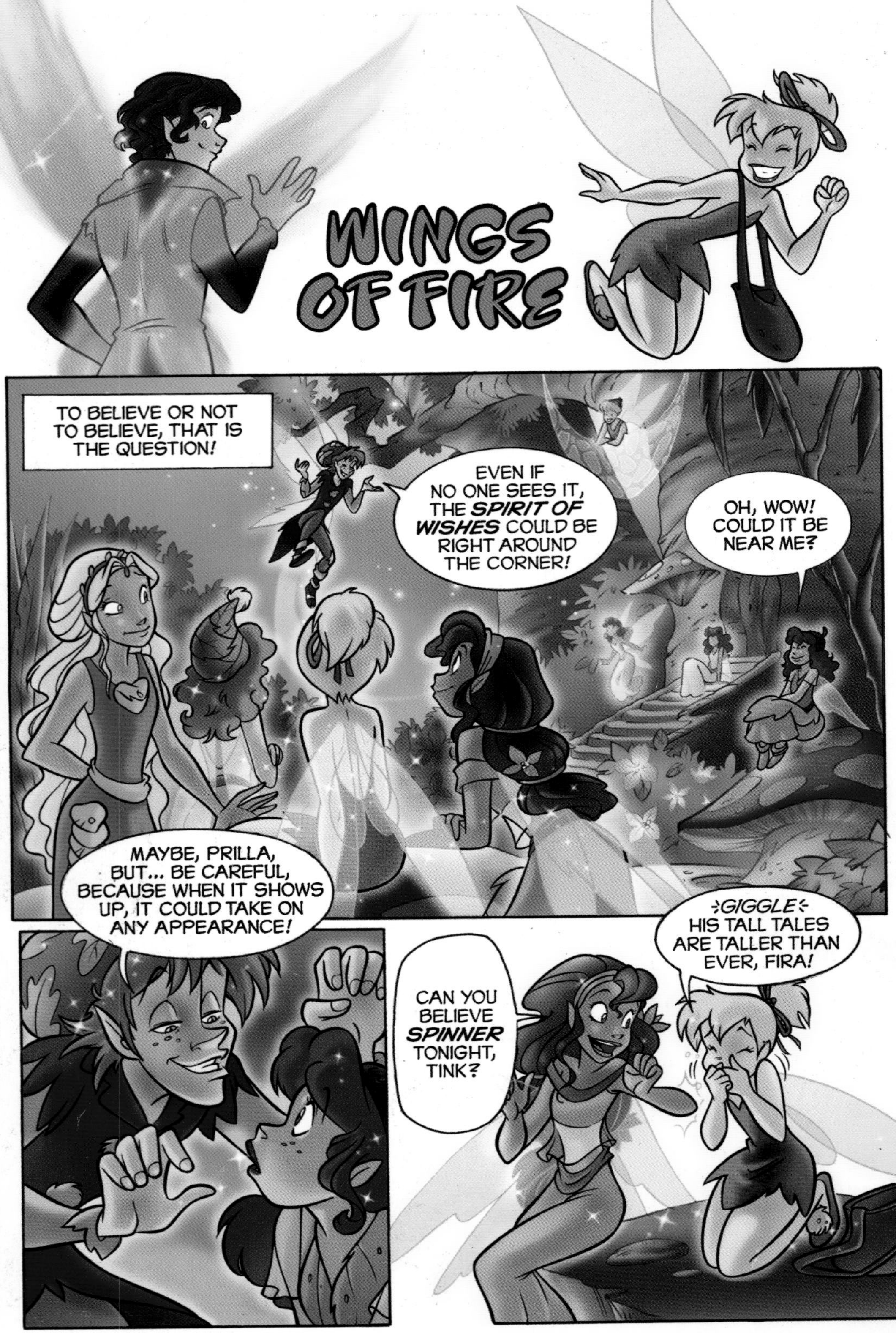
WINGS OF FIRE
TO BELIEVE OR NOT TO BELIEVE, THAT IS THE QUESTION!
EVEN IF NO ONE SEES IT, THE SPIRIT OF WISHES COULD BE RIGHT AROUND THE CORNER!
OH, WOW! COULD IT BE NEAR ME?
MAYBE, PRILLA, BUT... BE CAREFUL, BECAUSE WHEN IT SHOWS UP, IT COULD TAKE ON ANY APPEARANCE!
CAN YOU BELIEVE SPINNER TONIGHT, TINK?
GIGGLE
HIS TALL TALES ARE TALLER THAN EVER, FIRA!

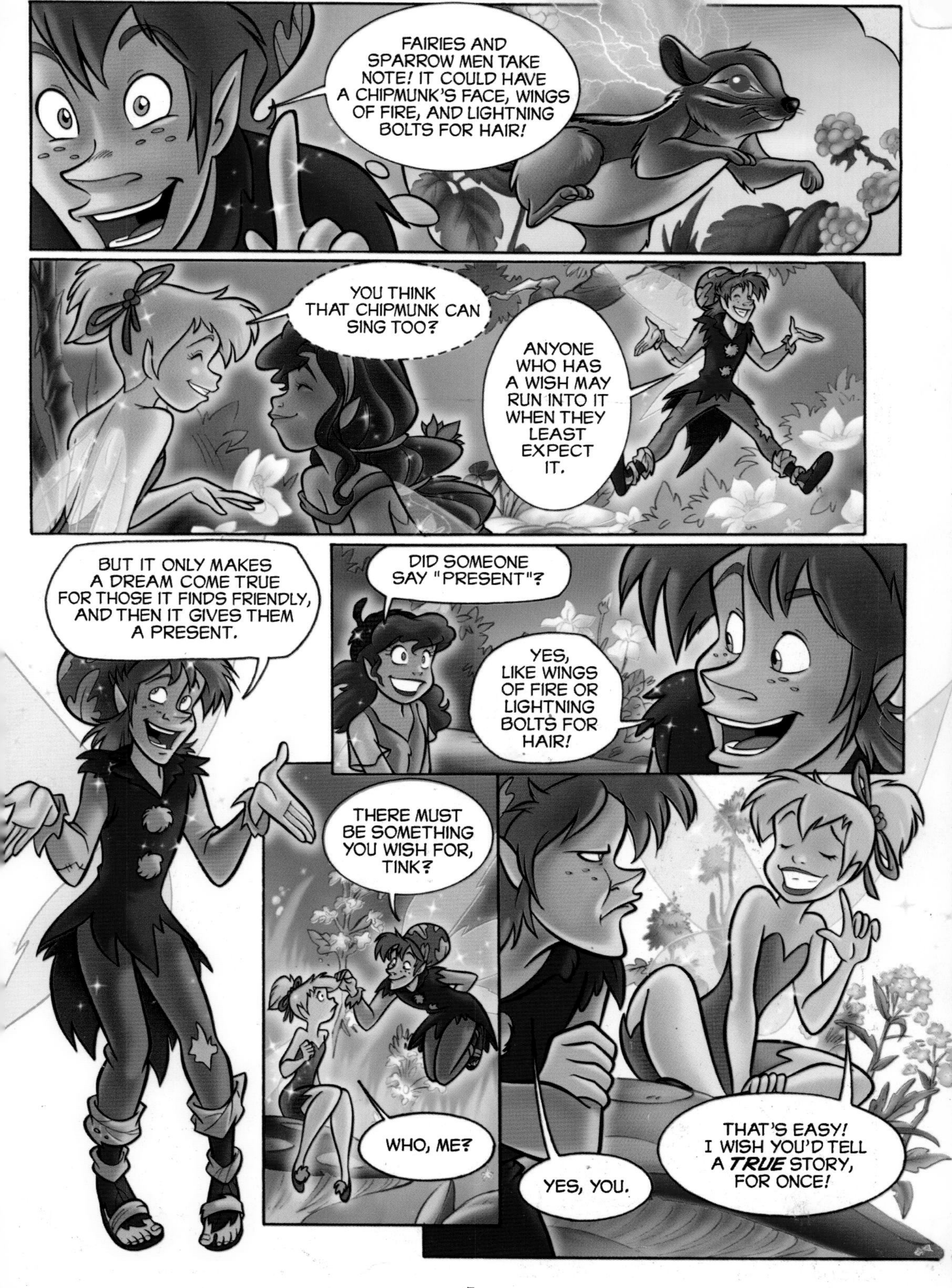
FAIRIES AND SPARROW MEN TAKE NOTE! IT COULD HAVE A CHIPMUNK'S FACE, WINGS OF FIRE, AND LIGHTNING BOLTS FOR HAIR!
YOU THINK THAT CHIPMUNK CAN SING TOO?
ANYONE WHO HAS A WISH MAY RUN INTO IT WHEN THEY LEAST EXPECT IT.
BUT IT ONLY MAKES A DREAM COME TRUE FOR THOSE IT FINDS FRIENDLY, AND THEN IT GIVES THEM A PRESENT.
DID SOMEONE SAY "PRESENT"?
YES, LIKE WINGS OF FIRE OR LIGHTNING BOLTS FOR HAIR!
THERE MUST BE SOMETHING YOU WISH FOR, TINK?
WHO, ME?
YES, YOU.
THAT'S EASY! I WISH YOU'D TELL A ***TRUE*** STORY, FOR ONCE!

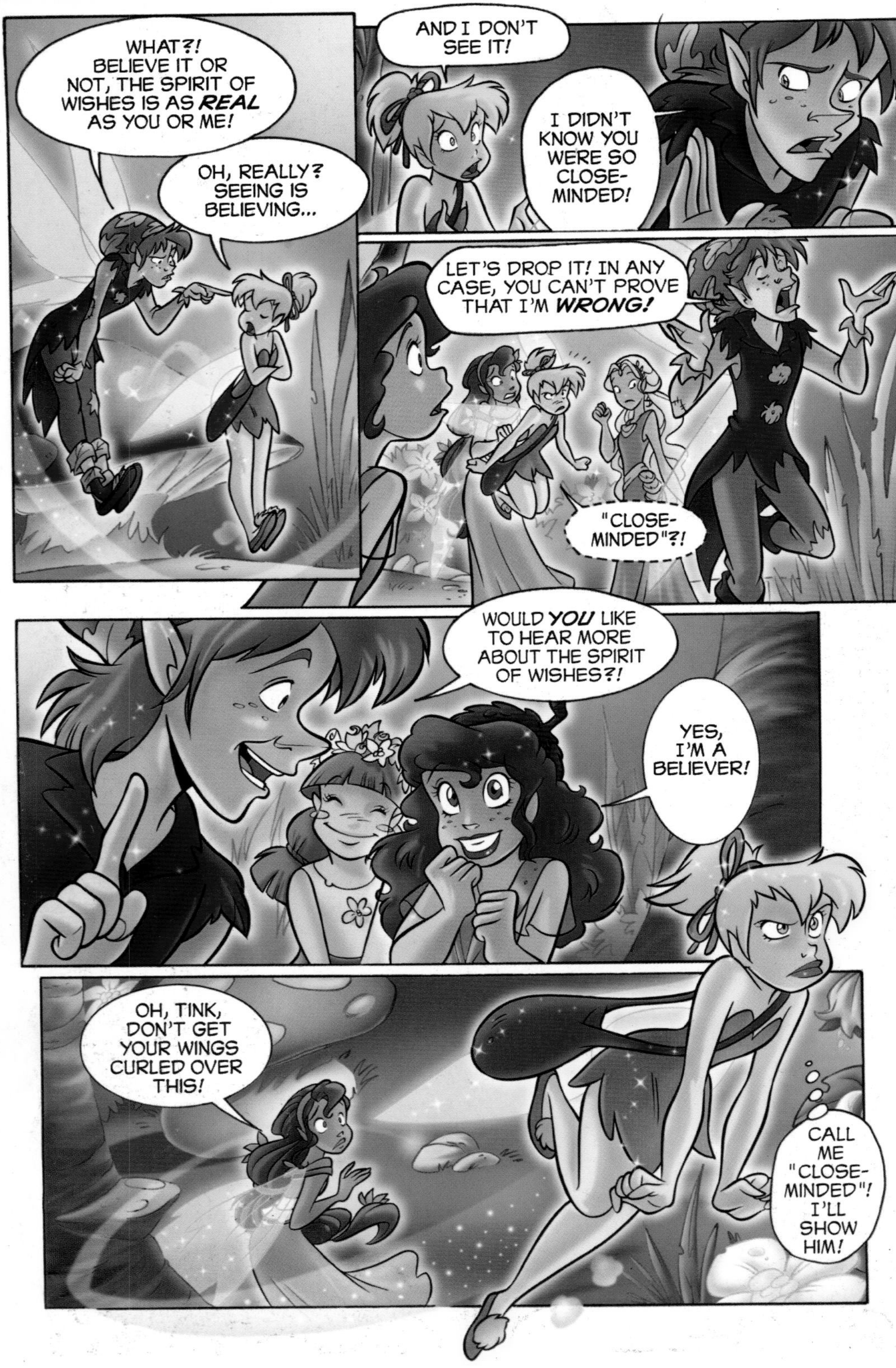
WHAT?! BELIEVE IT OR NOT, THE SPIRIT OF WISHES IS AS REAL AS YOU OR ME!
OH, REALLY? SEEING IS BELIEVING...
AND I DON'T SEE IT!
I DIDN'T KNOW YOU WERE SO CLOSE-MINDED!
LET'S DROP IT! IN ANY CASE, YOU CAN'T PROVE THAT I'M WRONG!
"CLOSE-MINDED"?!
WOULD YOU LIKE TO HEAR MORE ABOUT THE SPIRIT OF WISHES?!
YES, I'M A BELIEVER!
OH, TINK, DON'T GET YOUR WINGS CURLED OVER THIS!
CALL ME "CLOSE-MINDED"! I'LL SHOW HIM!

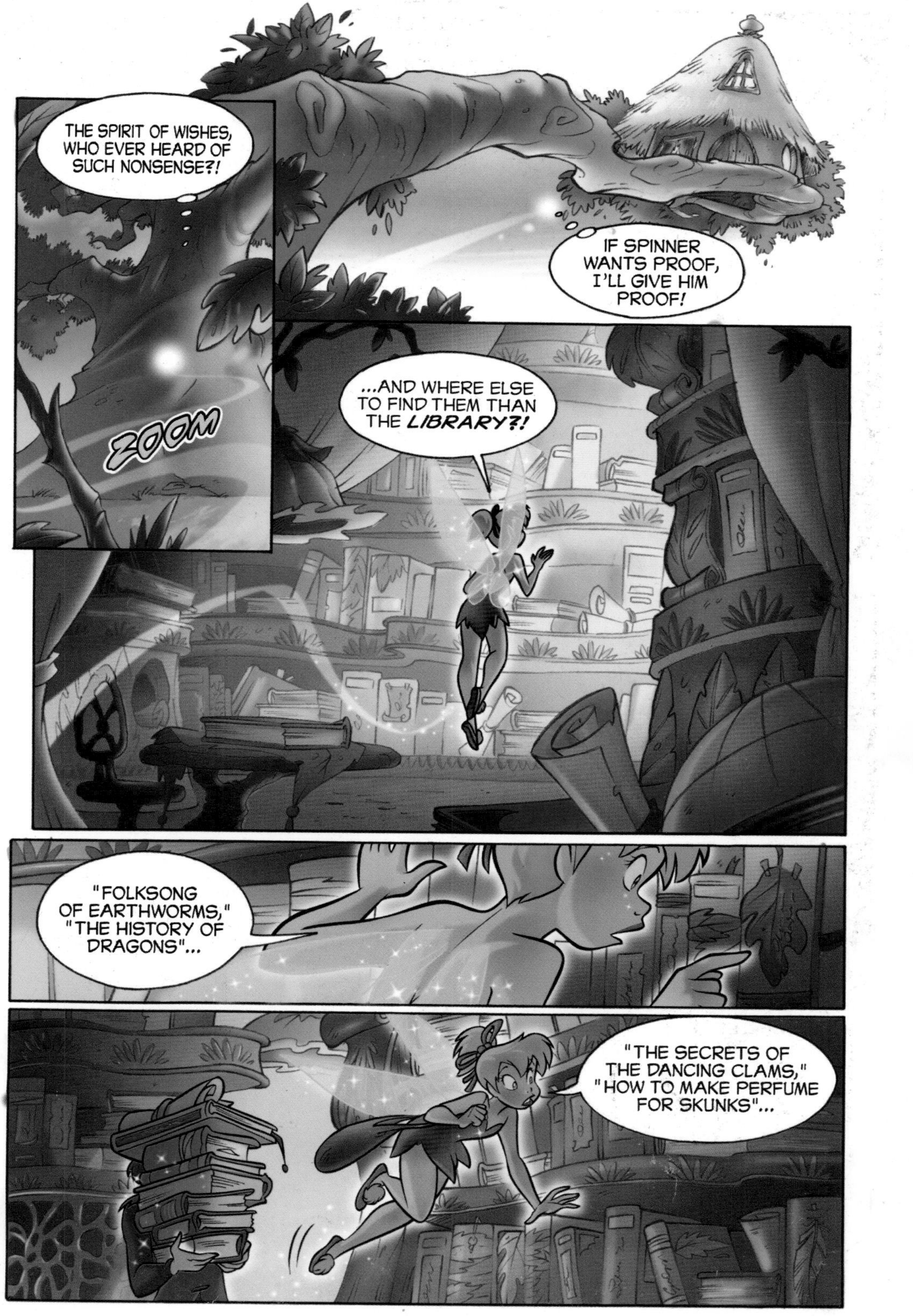
THE SPIRIT OF WISHES, WHO EVER HEARD OF SUCH NONSENSE?!
IF SPINNER WANTS PROOF, I'LL GIVE HIM PROOF!
ZOOM
...AND WHERE ELSE TO FIND THEM THAN THE *LIBRARY?!*
"FOLKSONG OF EARTHWORMS," "THE HISTORY OF DRAGONS"...
"THE SECRETS OF THE DANCING CLAMS," "HOW TO MAKE PERFUME FOR SKUNKS"...

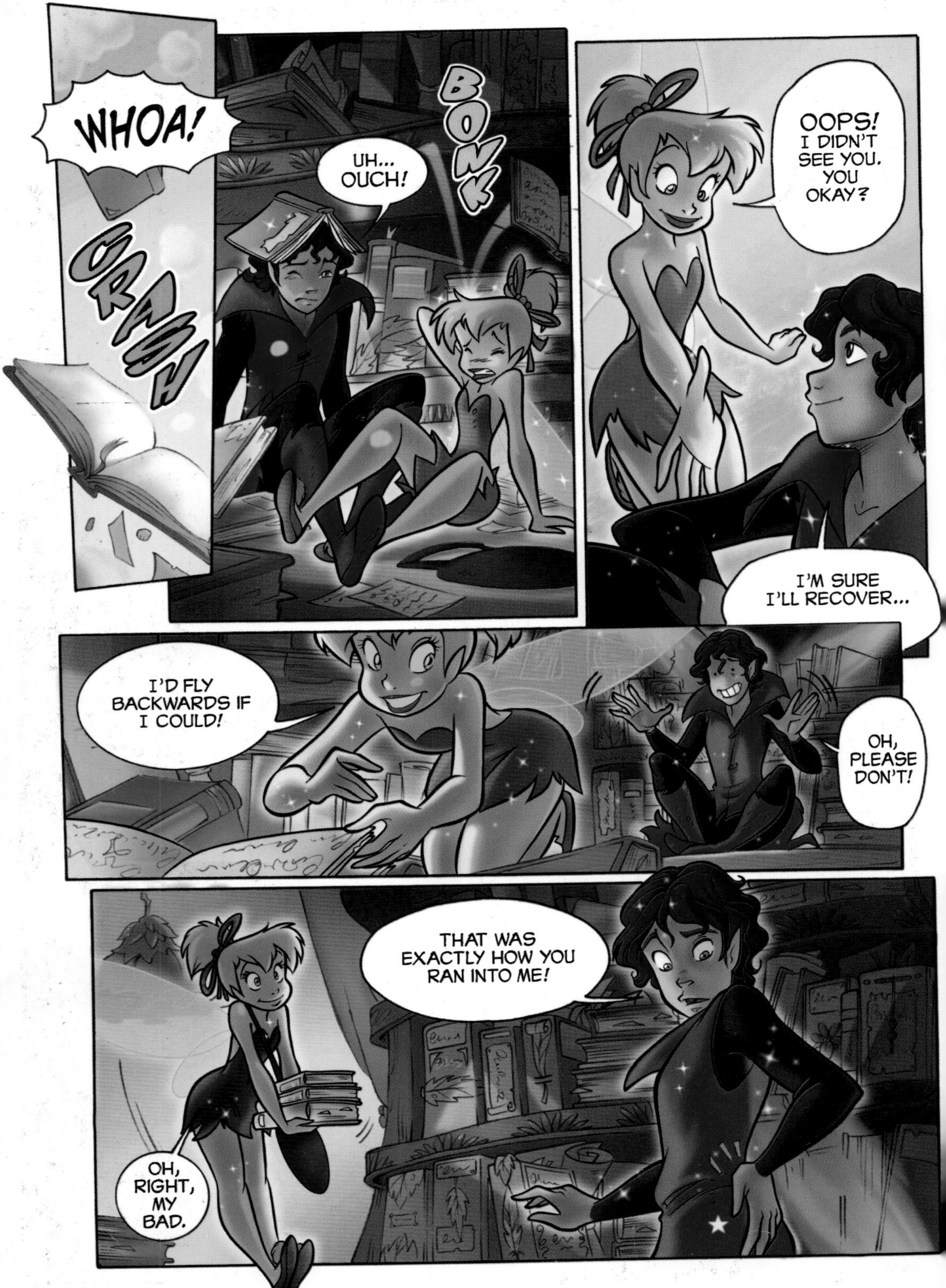
WHOA!
CRASH
UH... OUCH!
BONK
OOPS! I DIDN'T SEE YOU. YOU OKAY?
I'M SURE I'LL RECOVER...
I'D FLY BACKWARDS IF I COULD!
OH, PLEASE DON'T!
THAT WAS EXACTLY HOW YOU RAN INTO ME!
OH, RIGHT, MY BAD.

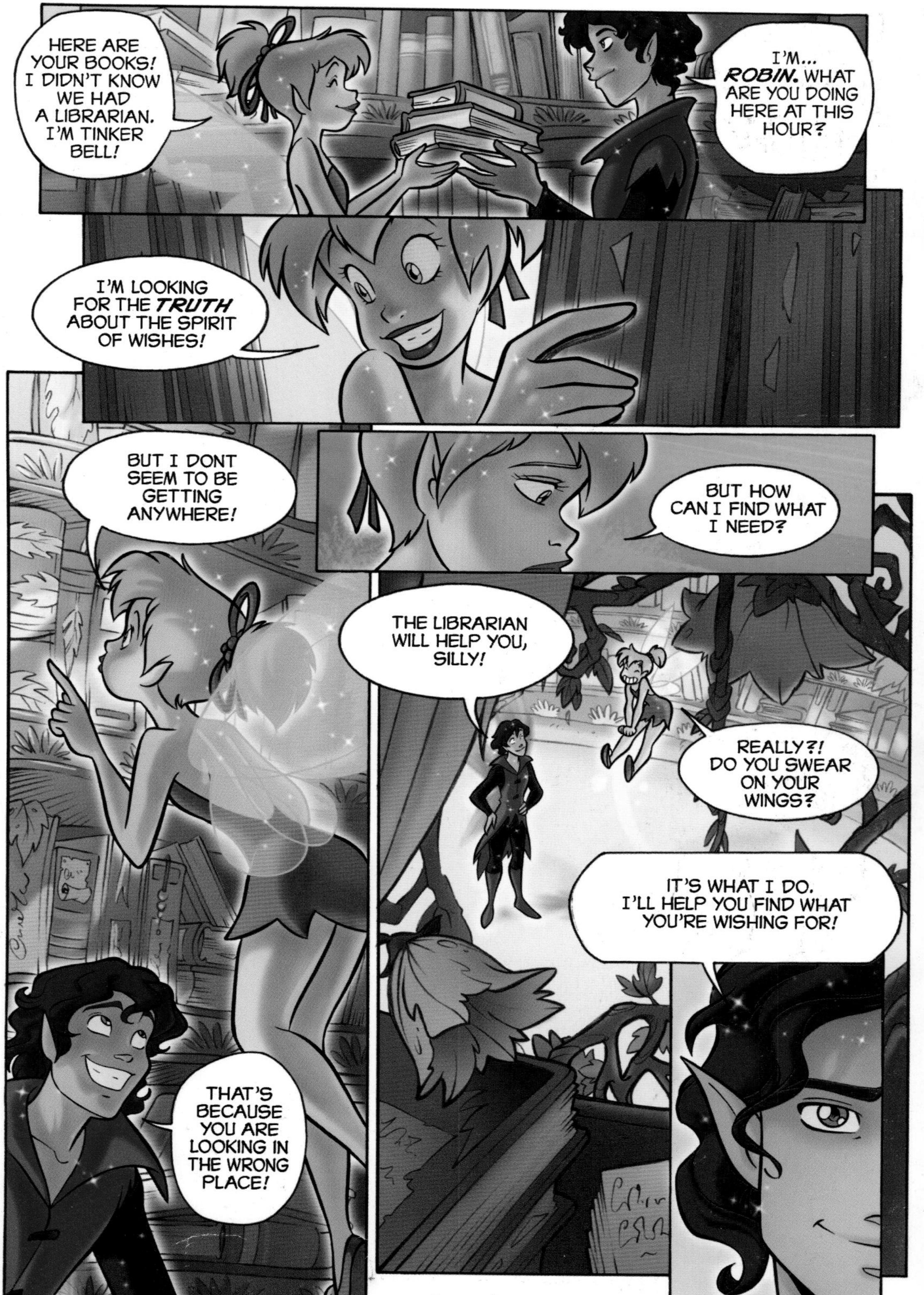
HERE ARE YOUR BOOKS! I DIDN'T KNOW WE HAD A LIBRARIAN. I'M TINKER BELL!
I'M... ROBIN. WHAT ARE YOU DOING HERE AT THIS HOUR?
I'M LOOKING FOR THE TRUTH ABOUT THE SPIRIT OF WISHES!
BUT I DONT SEEM TO BE GETTING ANYWHERE!
THAT'S BECAUSE YOU ARE LOOKING IN THE WRONG PLACE!
BUT HOW CAN I FIND WHAT I NEED?
THE LIBRARIAN WILL HELP YOU, SILLY!
REALLY?! DO YOU SWEAR ON YOUR WINGS?
IT'S WHAT I DO. I'LL HELP YOU FIND WHAT YOU'RE WISHING FOR!

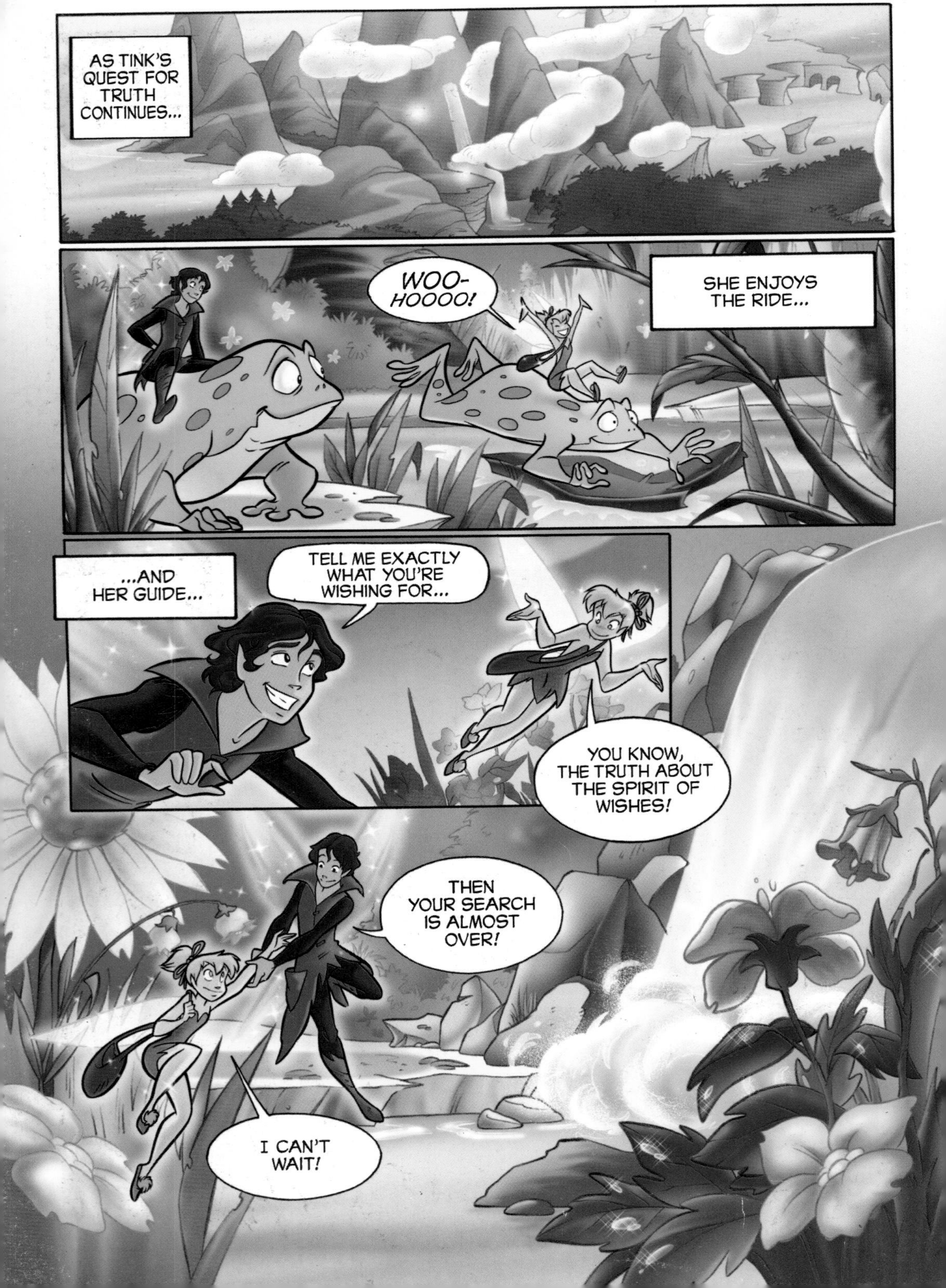

AS TINK'S QUEST FOR TRUTH CONTINUES...
WOO-HOOOOO!
SHE ENJOYS THE RIDE...
...AND HER GUIDE...
TELL ME EXACTLY WHAT YOU'RE WISHING FOR...
YOU KNOW, THE TRUTH ABOUT THE SPIRIT OF WISHES!
THEN YOUR SEARCH IS ALMOST OVER!
I CAN'T WAIT!

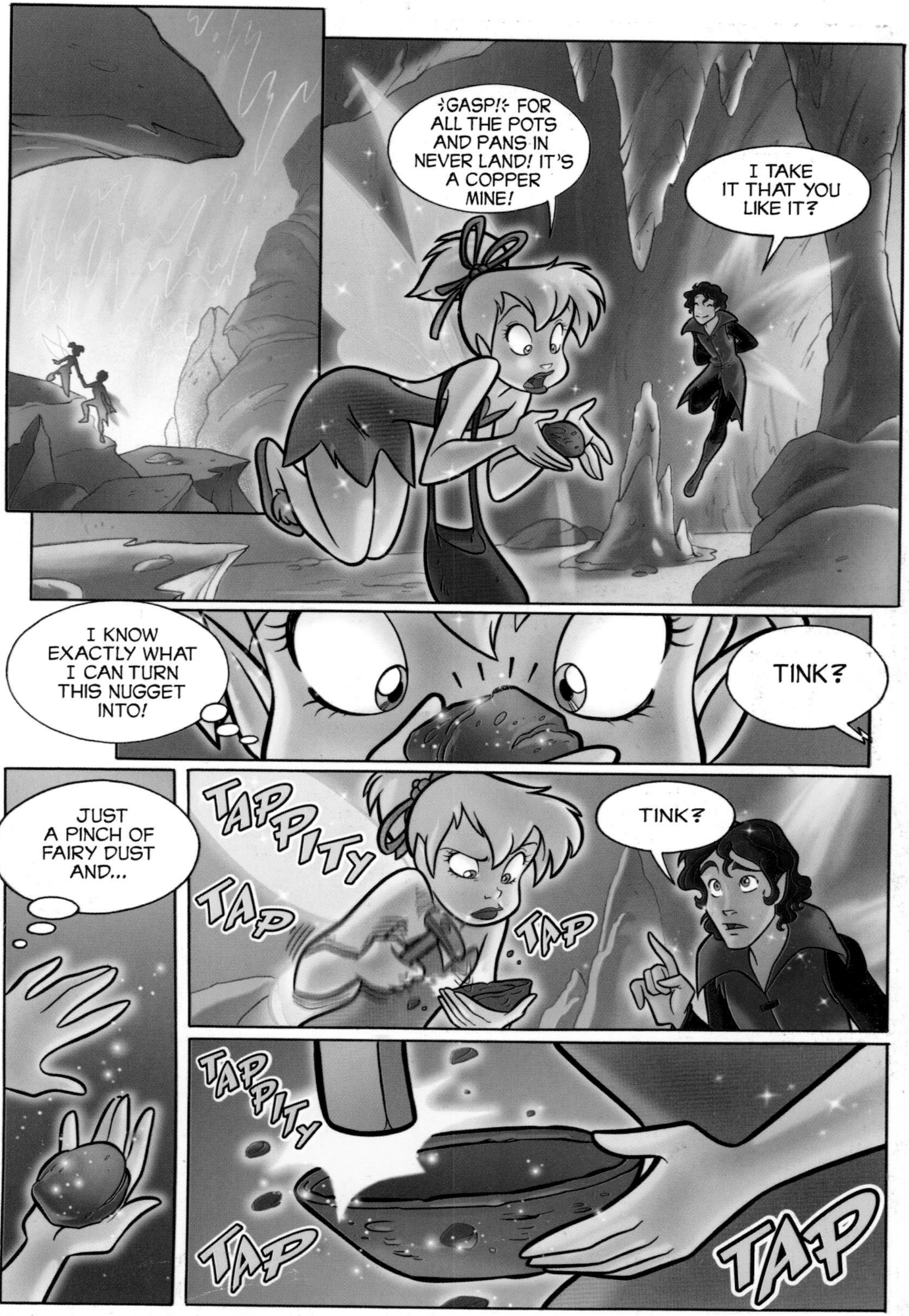
GASP! FOR ALL THE POTS AND PANS IN NEVER LAND! IT'S A COPPER MINE!
I TAKE IT THAT YOU LIKE IT?
I KNOW EXACTLY WHAT I CAN TURN THIS NUGGET INTO!
TINK?
JUST A PINCH OF FAIRY DUST AND...
TAPPITY
TAP
TAP
TINK?
TAPPITY
TAP
TAP

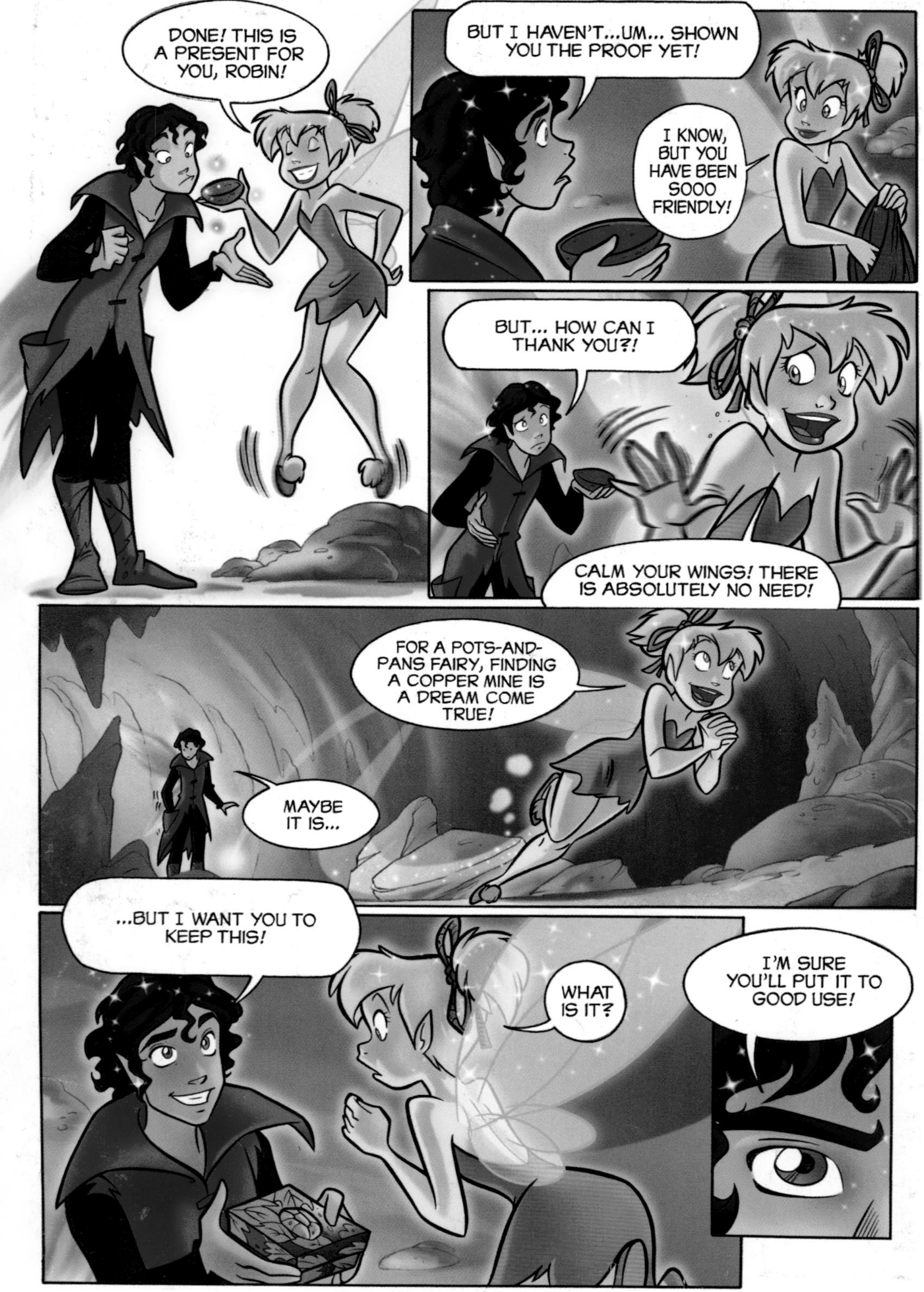
DONE! THIS IS A PRESENT FOR YOU, ROBIN!
BUT I HAVEN'T...UM... SHOWN YOU THE PROOF YET!
I KNOW, BUT YOU HAVE BEEN SOOO FRIENDLY!
BUT... HOW CAN I THANK YOU?!
CALM YOUR WINGS! THERE IS ABSOLUTELY NO NEED!
FOR A POTS-AND-PANS FAIRY, FINDING A COPPER MINE IS A DREAM COME TRUE!
MAYBE IT IS...
...BUT I WANT YOU TO KEEP THIS!
WHAT IS IT?
I'M SURE YOU'LL PUT IT TO GOOD USE!

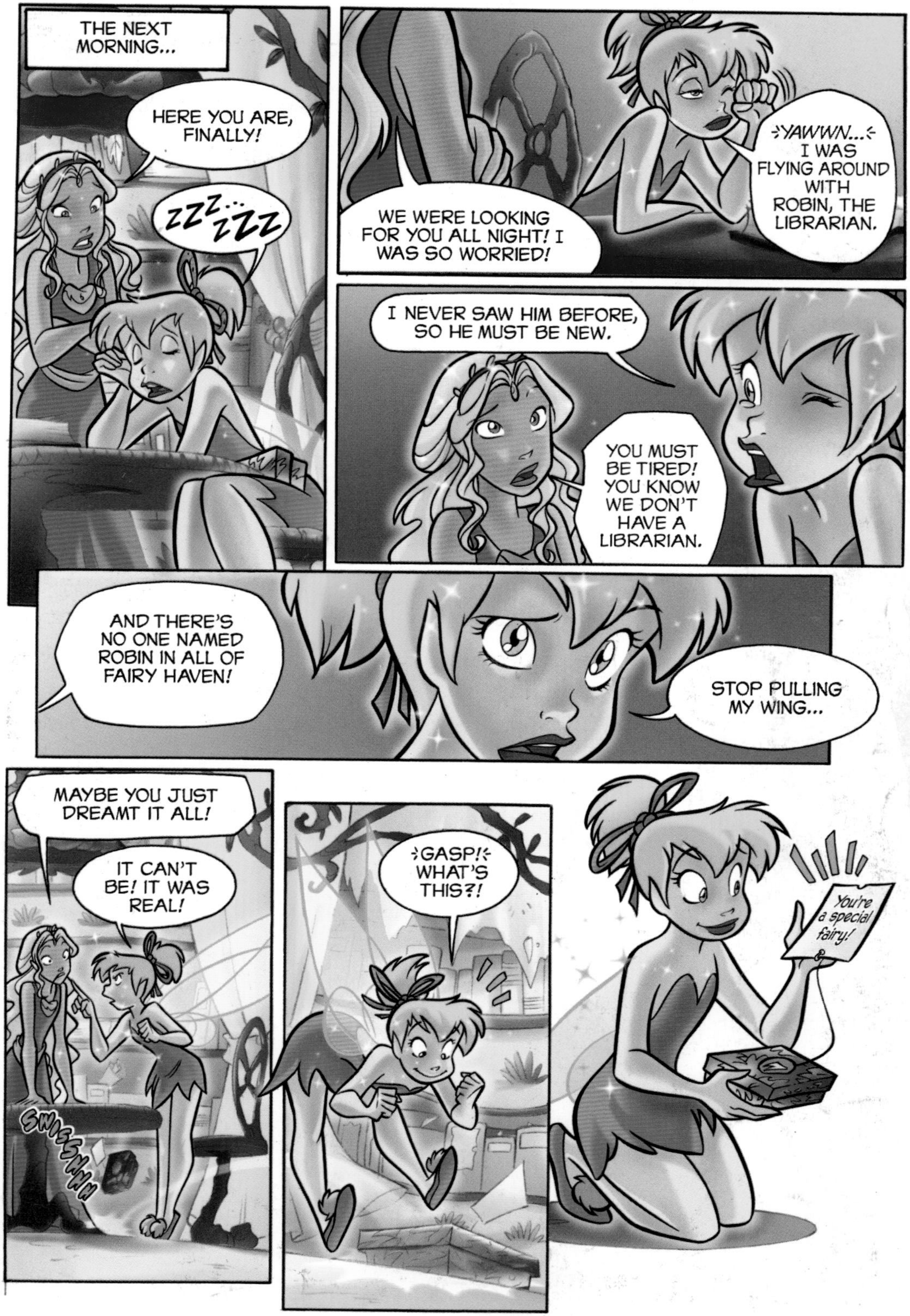
THE NEXT MORNING...
HERE YOU ARE, FINALLY!
ZZZ... ZZZ
WE WERE LOOKING FOR YOU ALL NIGHT! I WAS SO WORRIED!
YAWWN... I WAS FLYING AROUND WITH ROBIN, THE LIBRARIAN.
I NEVER SAW HIM BEFORE, SO HE MUST BE NEW.
YOU MUST BE TIRED! YOU KNOW WE DON'T HAVE A LIBRARIAN.
AND THERE'S NO ONE NAMED ROBIN IN ALL OF FAIRY HAVEN!
STOP PULLING MY WING...
MAYBE YOU JUST DREAMT IT ALL!
IT CAN'T BE! IT WAS REAL!
SWISSHHH
GASP! WHAT'S THIS?!
You're a special fairy!

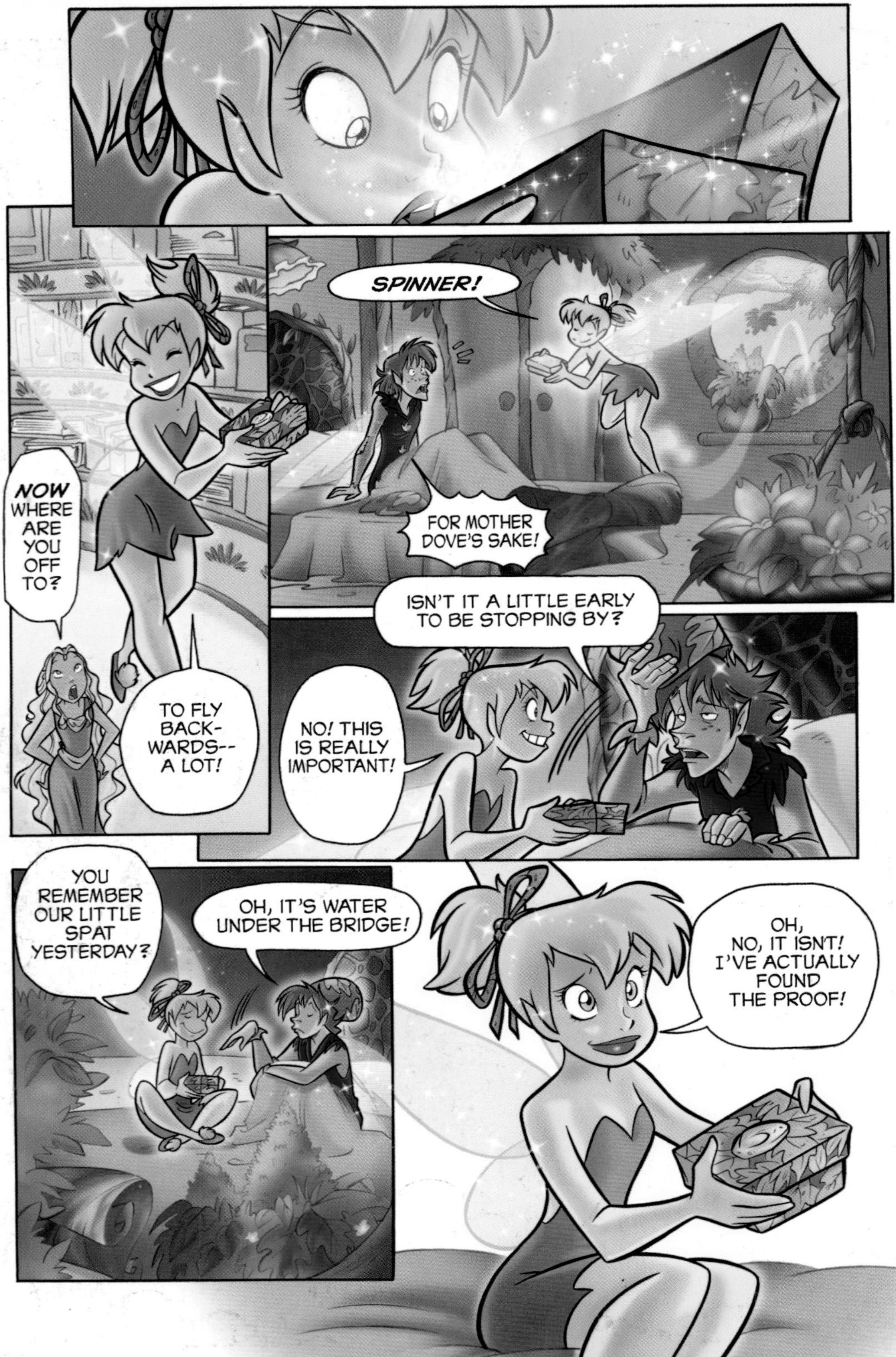

NOW WHERE ARE YOU OFF TO?
TO FLY BACK-WARDS-- A LOT!
SPINNER!
FOR MOTHER DOVE'S SAKE!
ISN'T IT A LITTLE EARLY TO BE STOPPING BY?
NO! THIS IS REALLY IMPORTANT!
YOU REMEMBER OUR LITTLE SPAT YESTERDAY?
OH, IT'S WATER UNDER THE BRIDGE!
OH, NO, IT ISN'T! I'VE ACTUALLY FOUND THE PROOF!

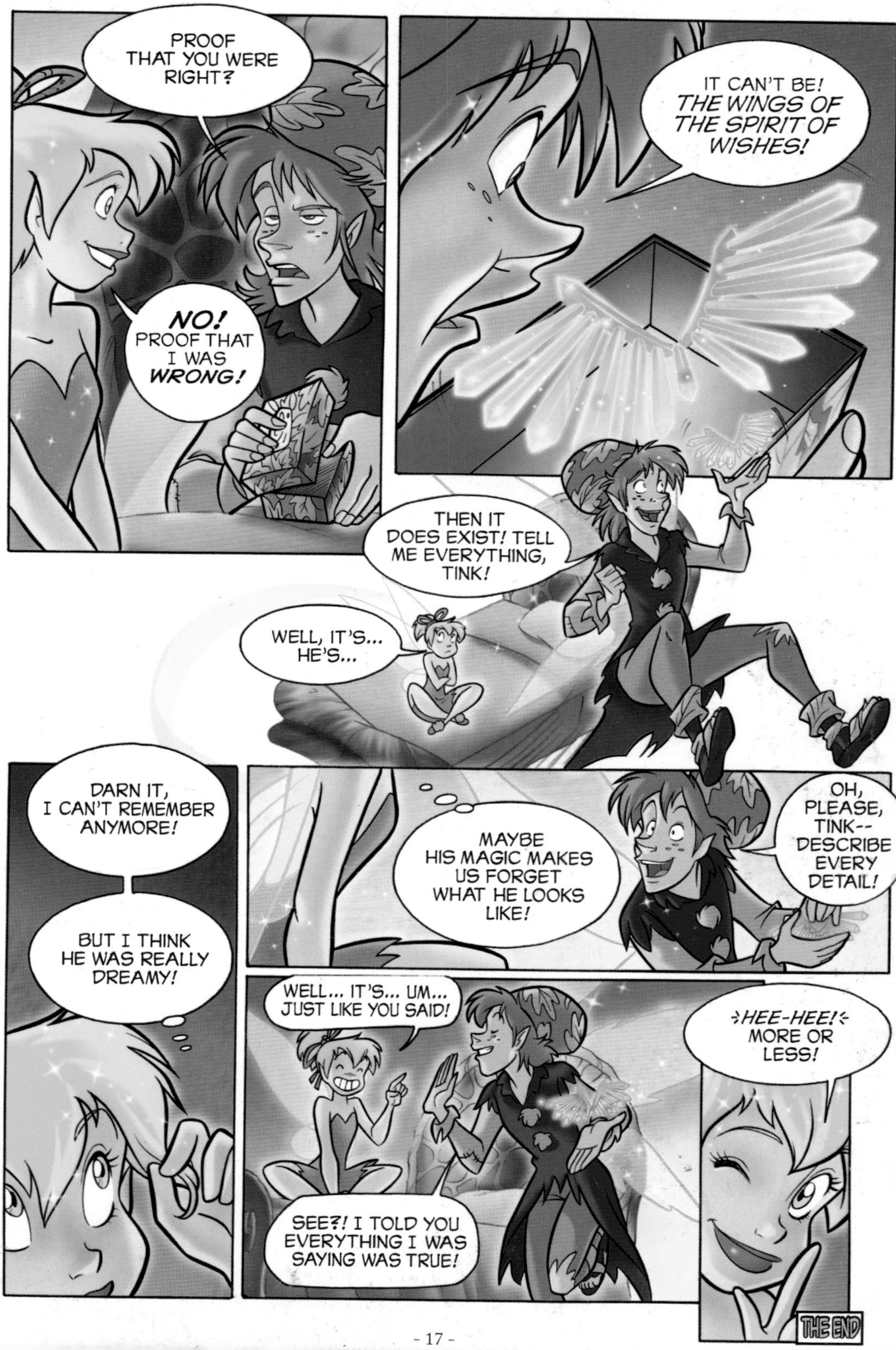
PROOF THAT YOU WERE RIGHT?
NO! PROOF THAT I WAS WRONG!
IT CAN'T BE! THE WINGS OF THE SPIRIT OF WISHES!
THEN IT DOES EXIST! TELL ME EVERYTHING, TINK!
WELL, IT'S... HE'S...
DARN IT, I CAN'T REMEMBER ANYMORE!
BUT I THINK HE WAS REALLY DREAMY!
MAYBE HIS MAGIC MAKES US FORGET WHAT HE LOOKS LIKE!
OH, PLEASE, TINK-- DESCRIBE EVERY DETAIL!
WELL... IT'S... UM... JUST LIKE YOU SAID!
SEE?! I TOLD YOU EVERYTHING I WAS SAYING WAS TRUE!
HEE-HEE! MORE OR LESS!
THE END

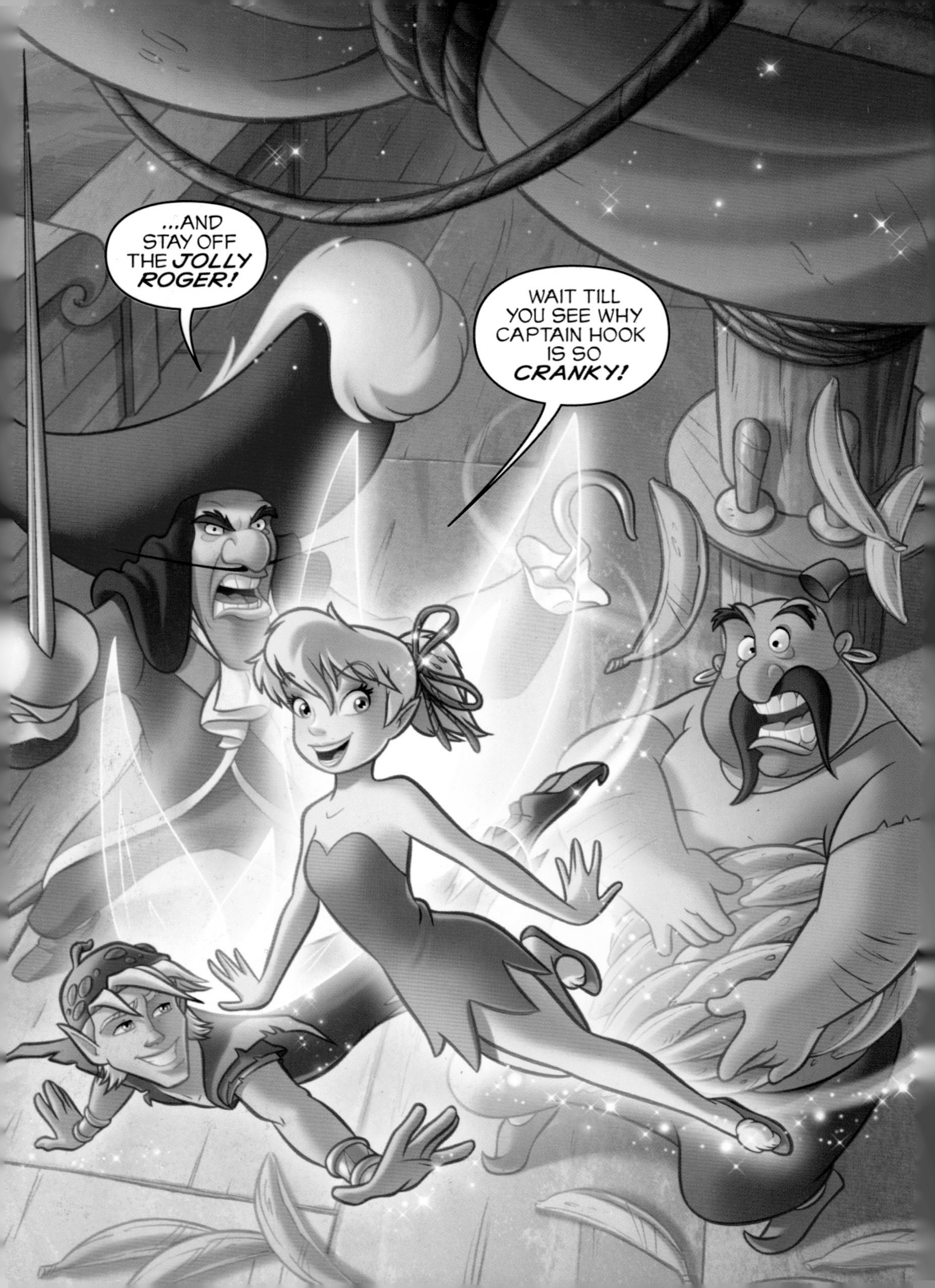
...AND STAY OFF THE JOLLY ROGER!
WAIT TILL YOU SEE WHY CAPTAIN HOOK IS SO CRANKY!

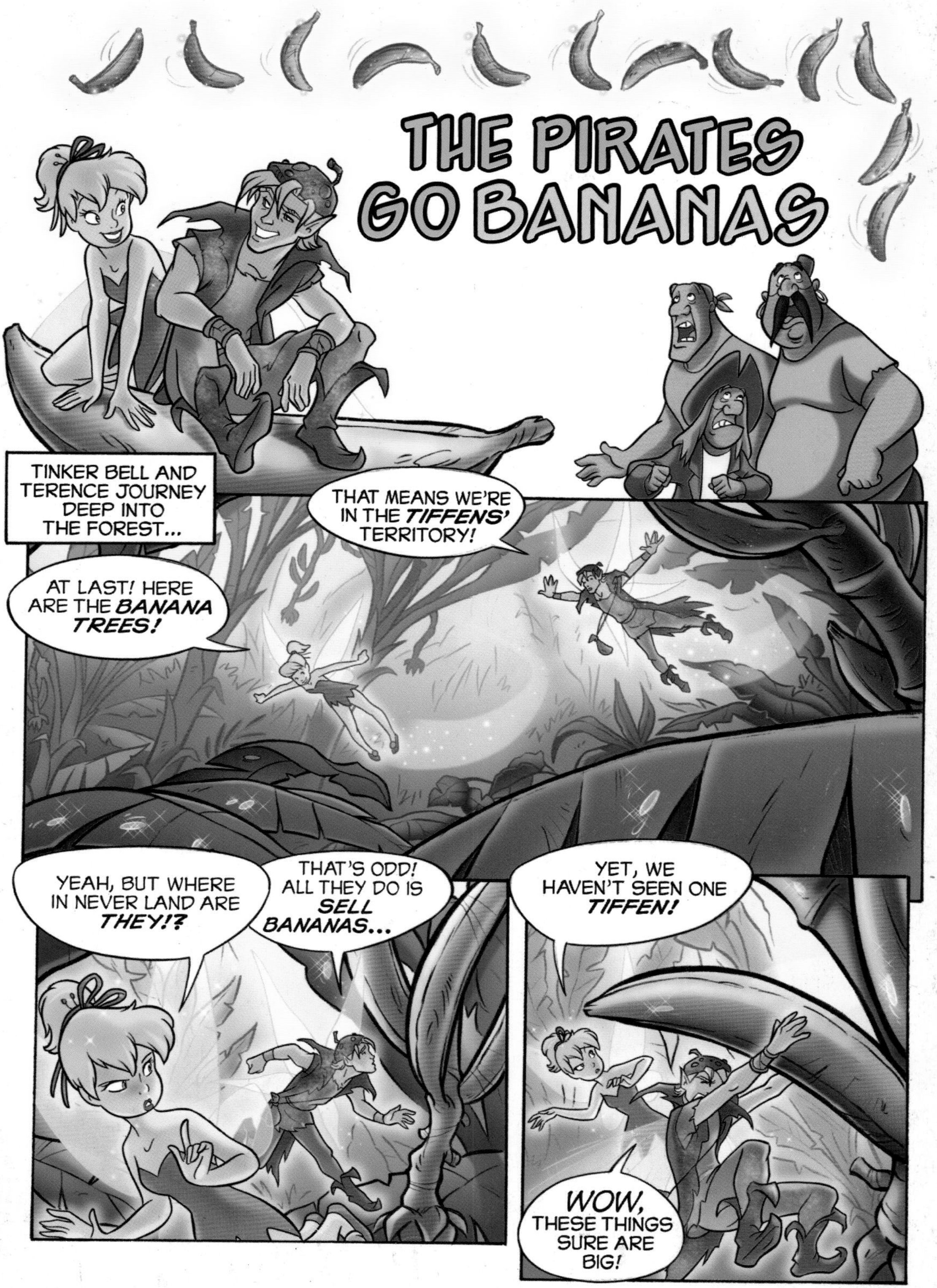
THE PIRATES GO BANANAS
TINKER BELL AND TERENCE JOURNEY DEEP INTO THE FOREST...
AT LAST! HERE ARE THE BANANA TREES!
THAT MEANS WE'RE IN THE TIFFENS' TERRITORY!
YEAH, BUT WHERE IN NEVER LAND ARE THEY!?
THAT'S ODD! ALL THEY DO IS SELL BANANAS...
YET, WE HAVEN'T SEEN ONE TIFFEN!
WOW, THESE THINGS SURE ARE BIG!

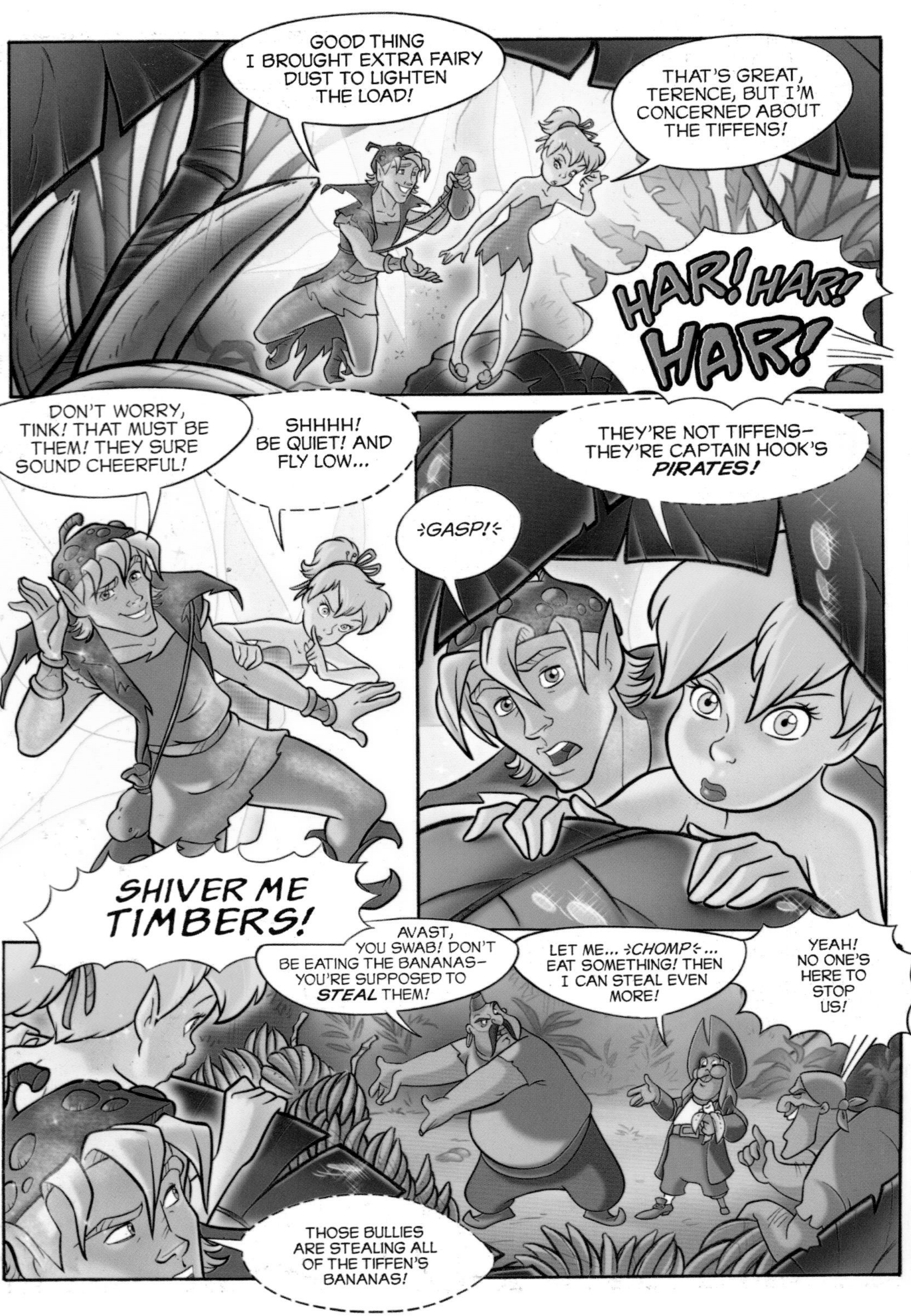
GOOD THING I BROUGHT EXTRA FAIRY DUST TO LIGHTEN THE LOAD!
THAT'S GREAT, TERENCE, BUT I'M CONCERNED ABOUT THE TIFFENS!
HAR! HAR! HAR!
DON'T WORRY, TINK! THAT MUST BE THEM! THEY SURE SOUND CHEERFUL!
SHHHH! BE QUIET! AND FLY LOW...
THEY'RE NOT TIFFENS– THEY'RE CAPTAIN HOOK'S PIRATES!
GASP!
SHIVER ME TIMBERS!
AVAST, YOU SWAB! DON'T BE EATING THE BANANAS– YOU'RE SUPPOSED TO STEAL THEM!
LET ME... CHOMP... EAT SOMETHING! THEN I CAN STEAL EVEN MORE!
YEAH! NO ONE'S HERE TO STOP US!
THOSE BULLIES ARE STEALING ALL OF THE TIFFEN'S BANANAS!

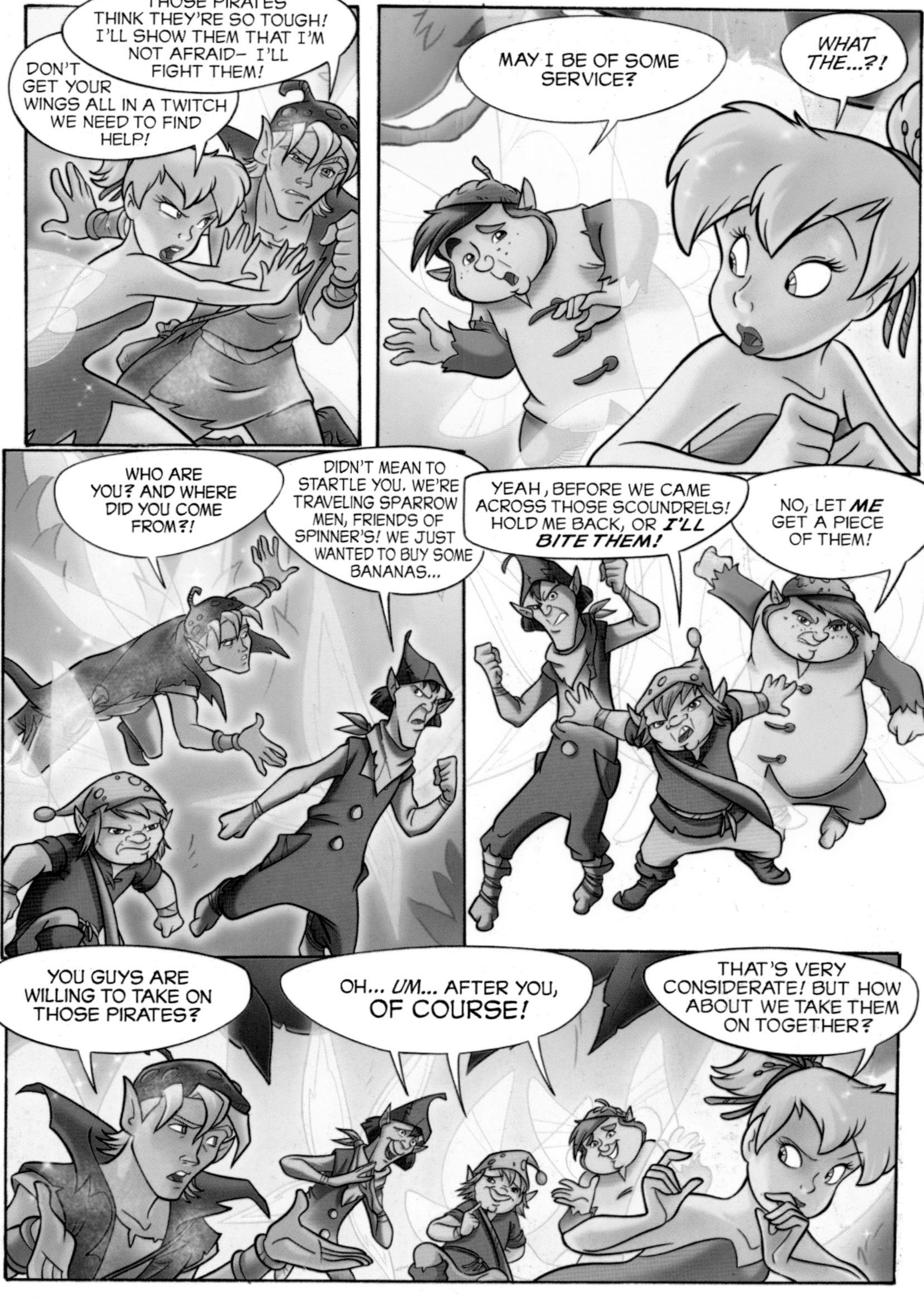
THOSE PIRATES THINK THEY'RE SO TOUGH! I'LL SHOW THEM THAT I'M NOT AFRAID– I'LL FIGHT THEM!
DON'T GET YOUR WINGS ALL IN A TWITCH WE NEED TO FIND HELP!
MAY I BE OF SOME SERVICE?
WHAT THE...?!
WHO ARE YOU? AND WHERE DID YOU COME FROM?!
DIDN'T MEAN TO STARTLE YOU. WE'RE TRAVELING SPARROW MEN, FRIENDS OF SPINNER'S! WE JUST WANTED TO BUY SOME BANANAS...
YEAH, BEFORE WE CAME ACROSS THOSE SCOUNDRELS! HOLD ME BACK, OR I'LL BITE THEM!
NO, LET ME GET A PIECE OF THEM!
YOU GUYS ARE WILLING TO TAKE ON THOSE PIRATES?
OH... UM... AFTER YOU, OF COURSE!
THAT'S VERY CONSIDERATE! BUT HOW ABOUT WE TAKE THEM ON TOGETHER?

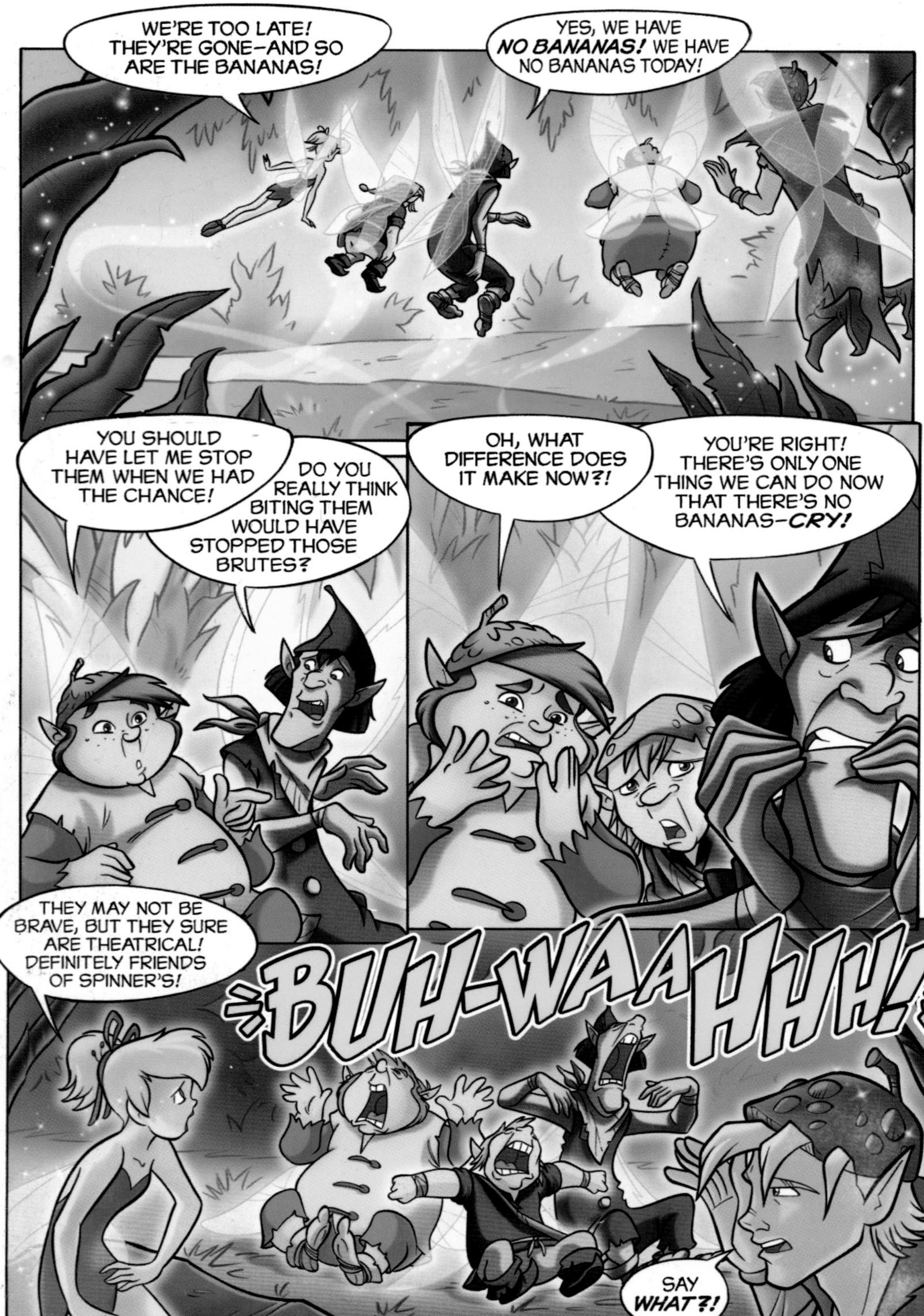
WE'RE TOO LATE! THEY'RE GONE–AND SO ARE THE BANANAS!
YES, WE HAVE NO BANANAS! WE HAVE NO BANANAS TODAY!
YOU SHOULD HAVE LET ME STOP THEM WHEN WE HAD THE CHANCE!
DO YOU REALLY THINK BITING THEM WOULD HAVE STOPPED THOSE BRUTES?
OH, WHAT DIFFERENCE DOES IT MAKE NOW?!
YOU'RE RIGHT! THERE'S ONLY ONE THING WE CAN DO NOW THAT THERE'S NO BANANAS–CRY!
THEY MAY NOT BE BRAVE, BUT THEY SURE ARE THEATRICAL! DEFINITELY FRIENDS OF SPINNER'S!
BUH-WAAAHHH!
SAY WHAT?!

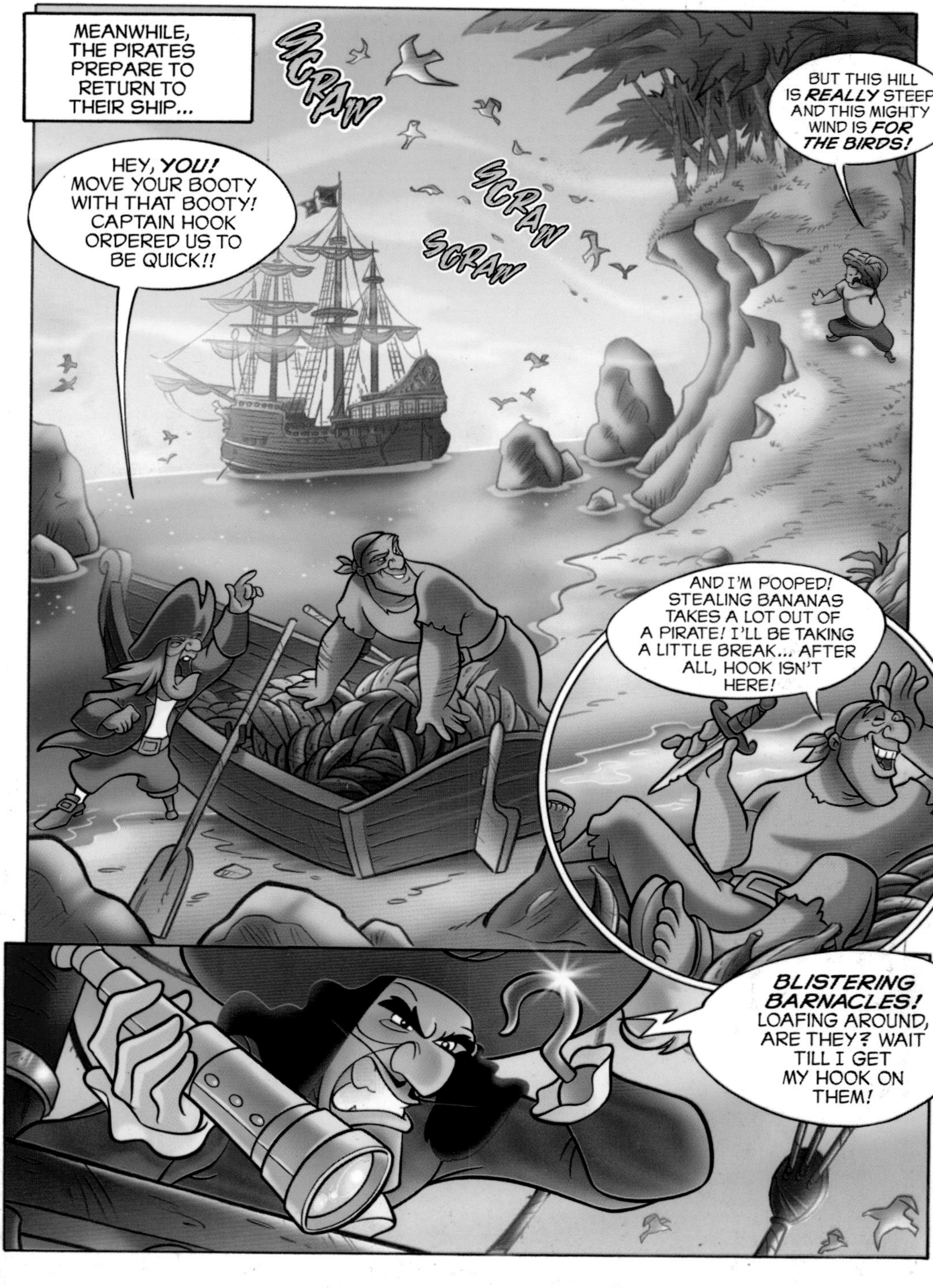
MEANWHILE, THE PIRATES PREPARE TO RETURN TO THEIR SHIP...
SCRAW
HEY, YOU! MOVE YOUR BOOTY WITH THAT BOOTY! CAPTAIN HOOK ORDERED US TO BE QUICK!!
SCRAW
SCRAW
BUT THIS HILL IS REALLY STEEP! AND THIS MIGHTY WIND IS FOR THE BIRDS!
AND I'M POOPED! STEALING BANANAS TAKES A LOT OUT OF A PIRATE! I'LL BE TAKING A LITTLE BREAK... AFTER ALL, HOOK ISN'T HERE!
BLISTERING BARNACLES! LOAFING AROUND, ARE THEY? WAIT TILL I GET MY HOOK ON THEM!

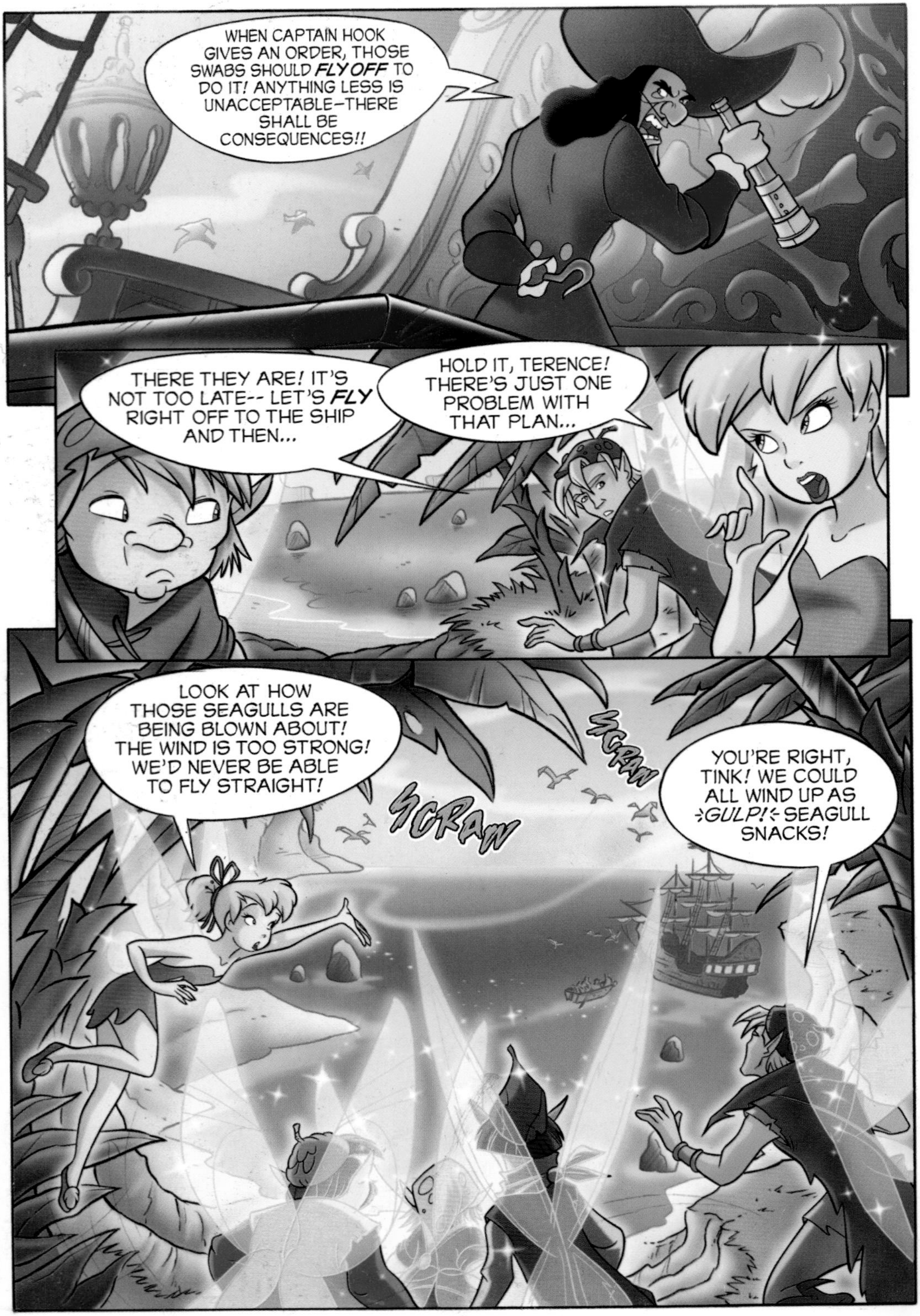
WHEN CAPTAIN HOOK GIVES AN ORDER, THOSE SWABS SHOULD *FLY OFF* TO DO IT! ANYTHING LESS IS UNACCEPTABLE–THERE SHALL BE CONSEQUENCES!!
THERE THEY ARE! IT'S NOT TOO LATE-- LET'S *FLY* RIGHT OFF TO THE SHIP AND THEN...
HOLD IT, TERENCE! THERE'S JUST ONE PROBLEM WITH THAT PLAN...
LOOK AT HOW THOSE SEAGULLS ARE BEING BLOWN ABOUT! THE WIND IS TOO STRONG! WE'D NEVER BE ABLE TO FLY STRAIGHT!
SCRAW
SCRAW
YOU'RE RIGHT, TINK! WE COULD ALL WIND UP AS *GULP!* SEAGULL SNACKS!

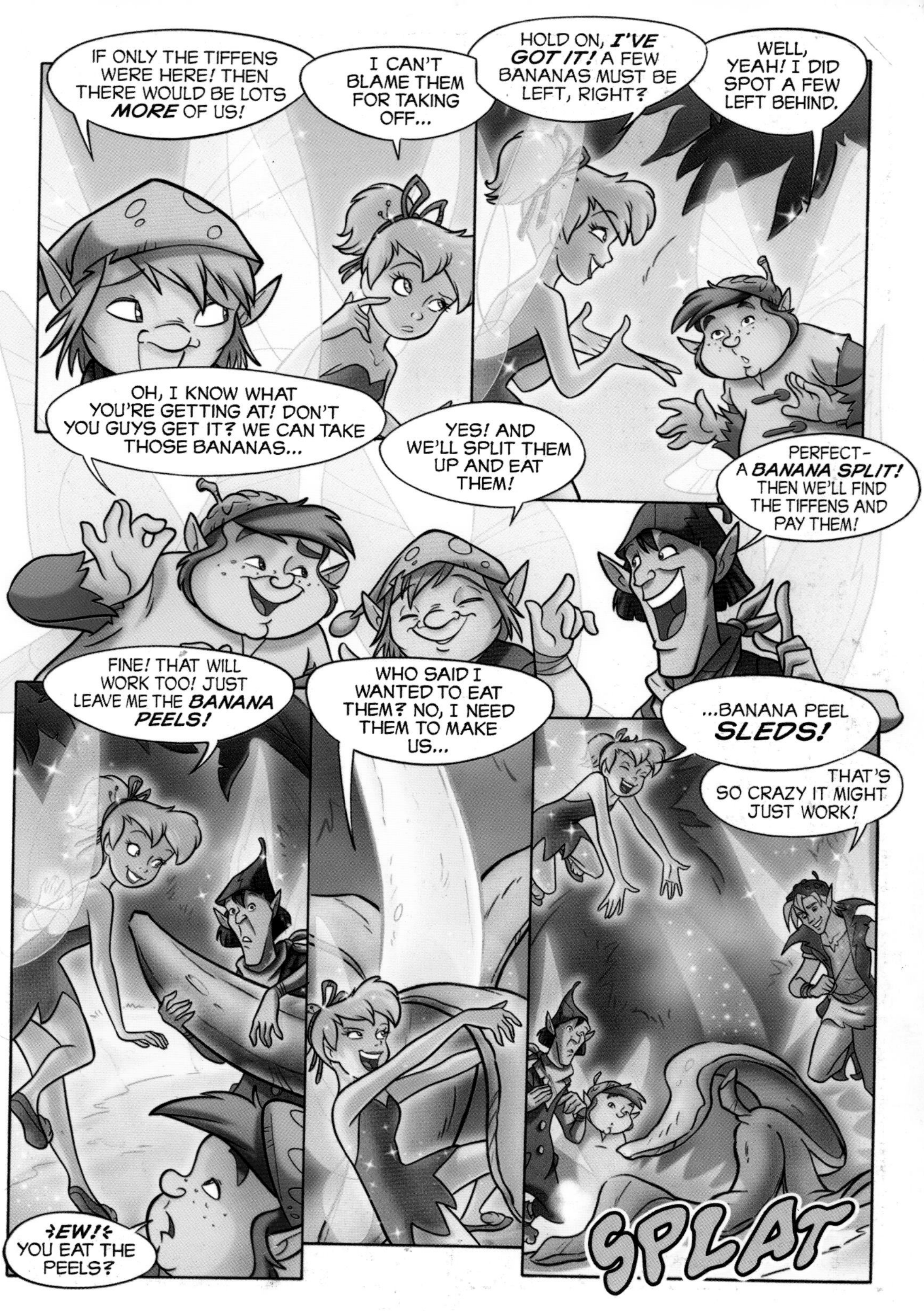
IF ONLY THE TIFFENS WERE HERE! THEN THERE WOULD BE LOTS MORE OF US!
I CAN'T BLAME THEM FOR TAKING OFF...
HOLD ON, I'VE GOT IT! A FEW BANANAS MUST BE LEFT, RIGHT?
WELL, YEAH! I DID SPOT A FEW LEFT BEHIND.
OH, I KNOW WHAT YOU'RE GETTING AT! DON'T YOU GUYS GET IT? WE CAN TAKE THOSE BANANAS...
YES! AND WE'LL SPLIT THEM UP AND EAT THEM!
PERFECT-A BANANA SPLIT! THEN WE'LL FIND THE TIFFENS AND PAY THEM!
FINE! THAT WILL WORK TOO! JUST LEAVE ME THE BANANA PEELS!
EW! YOU EAT THE PEELS?
WHO SAID I WANTED TO EAT THEM? NO, I NEED THEM TO MAKE US...
...BANANA PEEL SLEDS!
THAT'S SO CRAZY IT MIGHT JUST WORK!
SPLAT

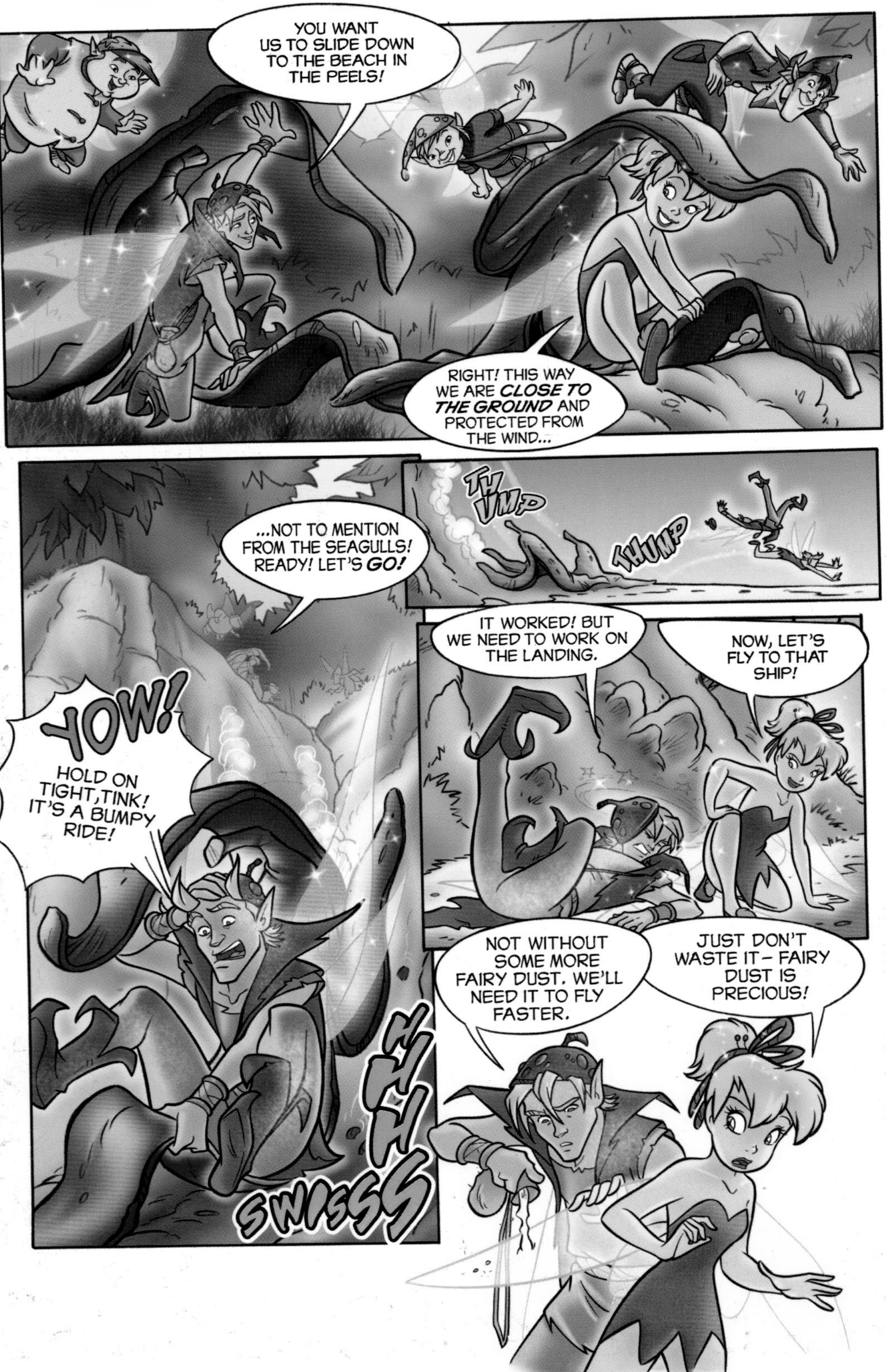
YOU WANT US TO SLIDE DOWN TO THE BEACH IN THE PEELS!
RIGHT! THIS WAY WE ARE CLOSE TO THE GROUND AND PROTECTED FROM THE WIND...
...NOT TO MENTION FROM THE SEAGULLS! READY! LET'S GO!
YOW!
HOLD ON TIGHT,TINK! IT'S A BUMPY RIDE!
SWISSS
THUMP
THUMP
IT WORKED! BUT WE NEED TO WORK ON THE LANDING.
NOW, LET'S FLY TO THAT SHIP!
NOT WITHOUT SOME MORE FAIRY DUST. WE'LL NEED IT TO FLY FASTER.
JUST DON'T WASTE IT– FAIRY DUST IS PRECIOUS!

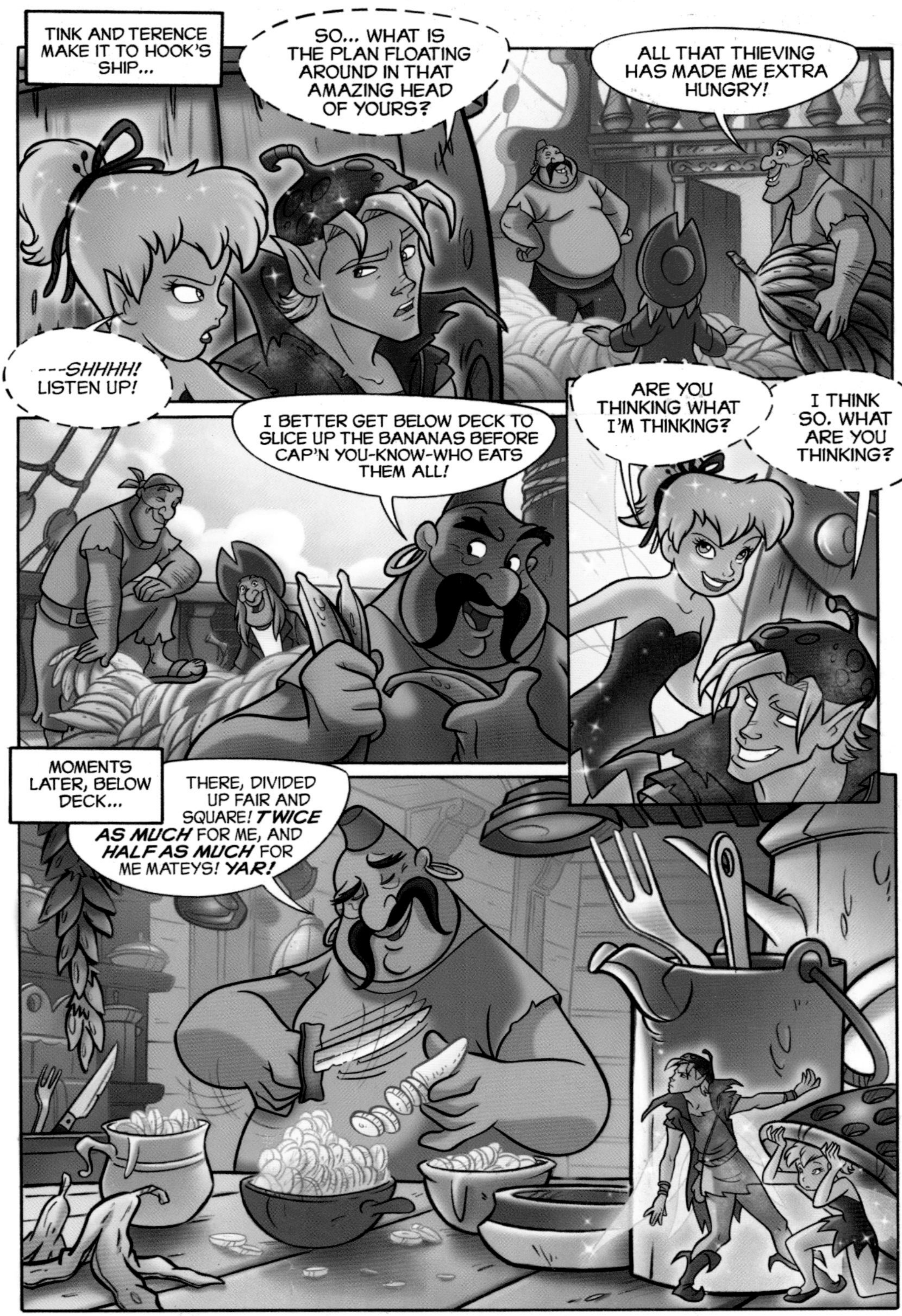
TINK AND TERENCE MAKE IT TO HOOK'S SHIP...
SO... WHAT IS THE PLAN FLOATING AROUND IN THAT AMAZING HEAD OF YOURS?
---SHHHH! LISTEN UP!
ALL THAT THIEVING HAS MADE ME EXTRA HUNGRY!
I BETTER GET BELOW DECK TO SLICE UP THE BANANAS BEFORE CAP'N YOU-KNOW-WHO EATS THEM ALL!
ARE YOU THINKING WHAT I'M THINKING?
I THINK SO. WHAT ARE YOU THINKING?
MOMENTS LATER, BELOW DECK...
THERE, DIVIDED UP FAIR AND SQUARE! TWICE AS MUCH FOR ME, AND HALF AS MUCH FOR ME MATEYS! YAR!

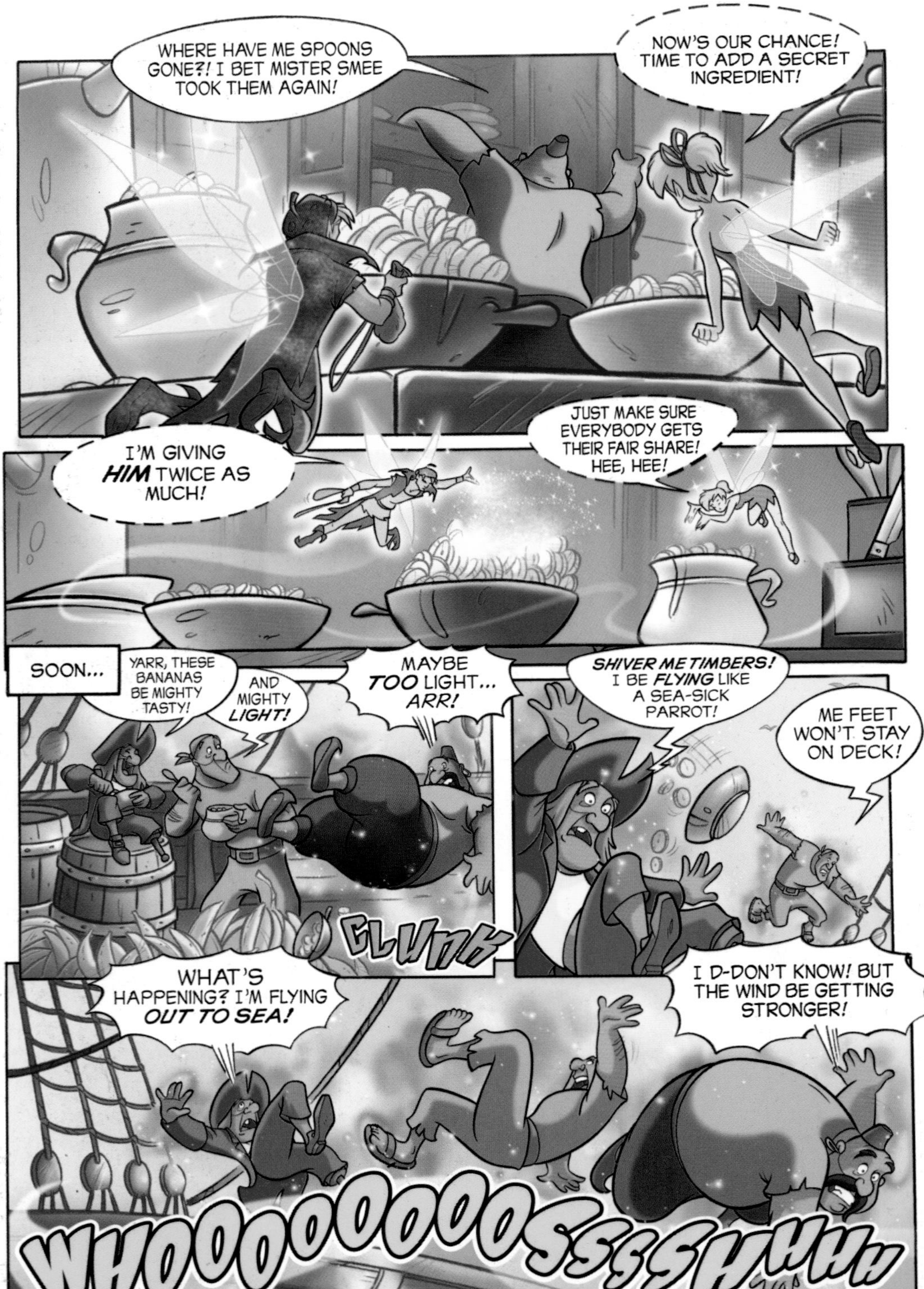
WHERE HAVE ME SPOONS GONE?! I BET MISTER SMEE TOOK THEM AGAIN!
NOW'S OUR CHANCE! TIME TO ADD A SECRET INGREDIENT!
I'M GIVING HIM TWICE AS MUCH!
JUST MAKE SURE EVERYBODY GETS THEIR FAIR SHARE! HEE, HEE!
SOON...
YARR, THESE BANANAS BE MIGHTY TASTY!
AND MIGHTY LIGHT!
MAYBE TOO LIGHT... ARR!
CLUNK
SHIVER ME TIMBERS! I BE FLYING LIKE A SEA-SICK PARROT!
ME FEET WON'T STAY ON DECK!
WHAT'S HAPPENING? I'M FLYING OUT TO SEA!
I D-DON'T KNOW! BUT THE WIND BE GETTING STRONGER!
WHOOOOOOOOSSSSHHHH

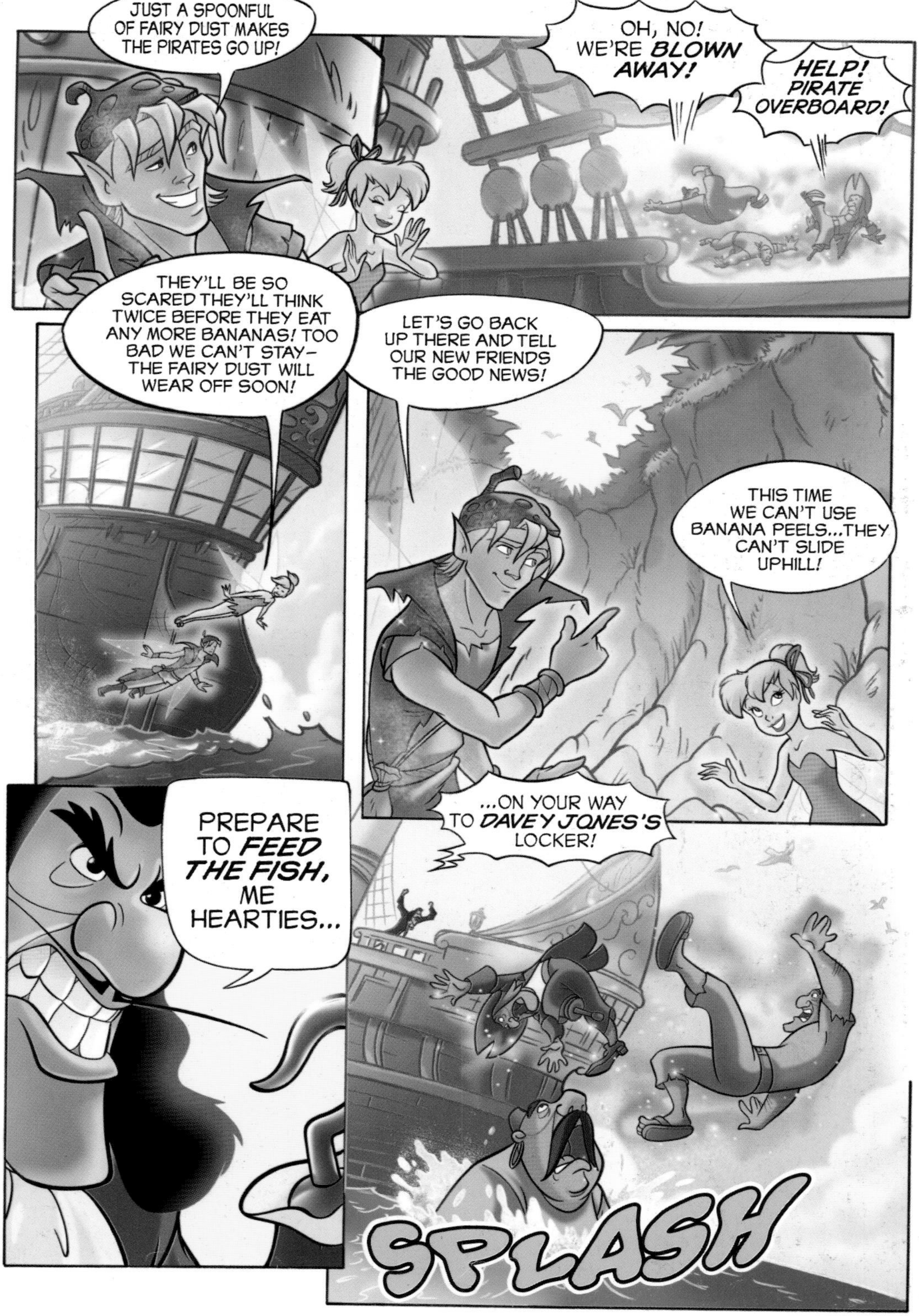
JUST A SPOONFUL OF FAIRY DUST MAKES THE PIRATES GO UP!
OH, NO! WE'RE BLOWN AWAY!
HELP! PIRATE OVERBOARD!
THEY'LL BE SO SCARED THEY'LL THINK TWICE BEFORE THEY EAT ANY MORE BANANAS! TOO BAD WE CAN'T STAY– THE FAIRY DUST WILL WEAR OFF SOON!
LET'S GO BACK UP THERE AND TELL OUR NEW FRIENDS THE GOOD NEWS!
THIS TIME WE CAN'T USE BANANA PEELS...THEY CAN'T SLIDE UPHILL!
PREPARE TO FEED THE FISH, ME HEARTIES...
...ON YOUR WAY TO DAVEY JONES'S LOCKER!
SPLASH

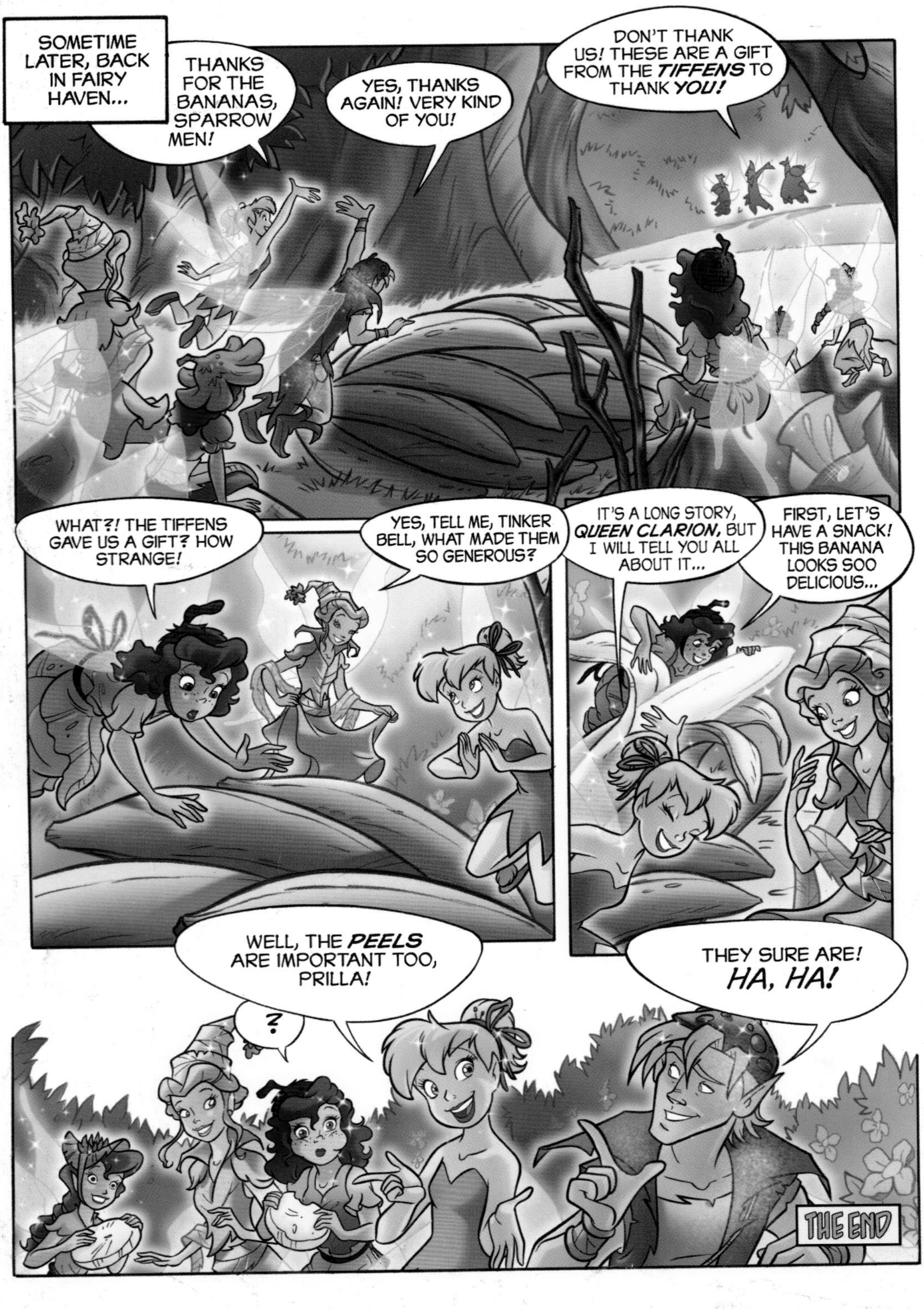
SOMETIME LATER, BACK IN FAIRY HAVEN...
THANKS FOR THE BANANAS, SPARROW MEN!
YES, THANKS AGAIN! VERY KIND OF YOU!
DON'T THANK US! THESE ARE A GIFT FROM THE TIFFENS TO THANK YOU!
WHAT?! THE TIFFENS GAVE US A GIFT? HOW STRANGE!
YES, TELL ME, TINKER BELL, WHAT MADE THEM SO GENEROUS?
IT'S A LONG STORY, QUEEN CLARION, BUT I WILL TELL YOU ALL ABOUT IT...
FIRST, LET'S HAVE A SNACK! THIS BANANA LOOKS SOO DELICIOUS...
WELL, THE PEELS ARE IMPORTANT TOO, PRILLA!
?
THEY SURE ARE! HA, HA!
THE END

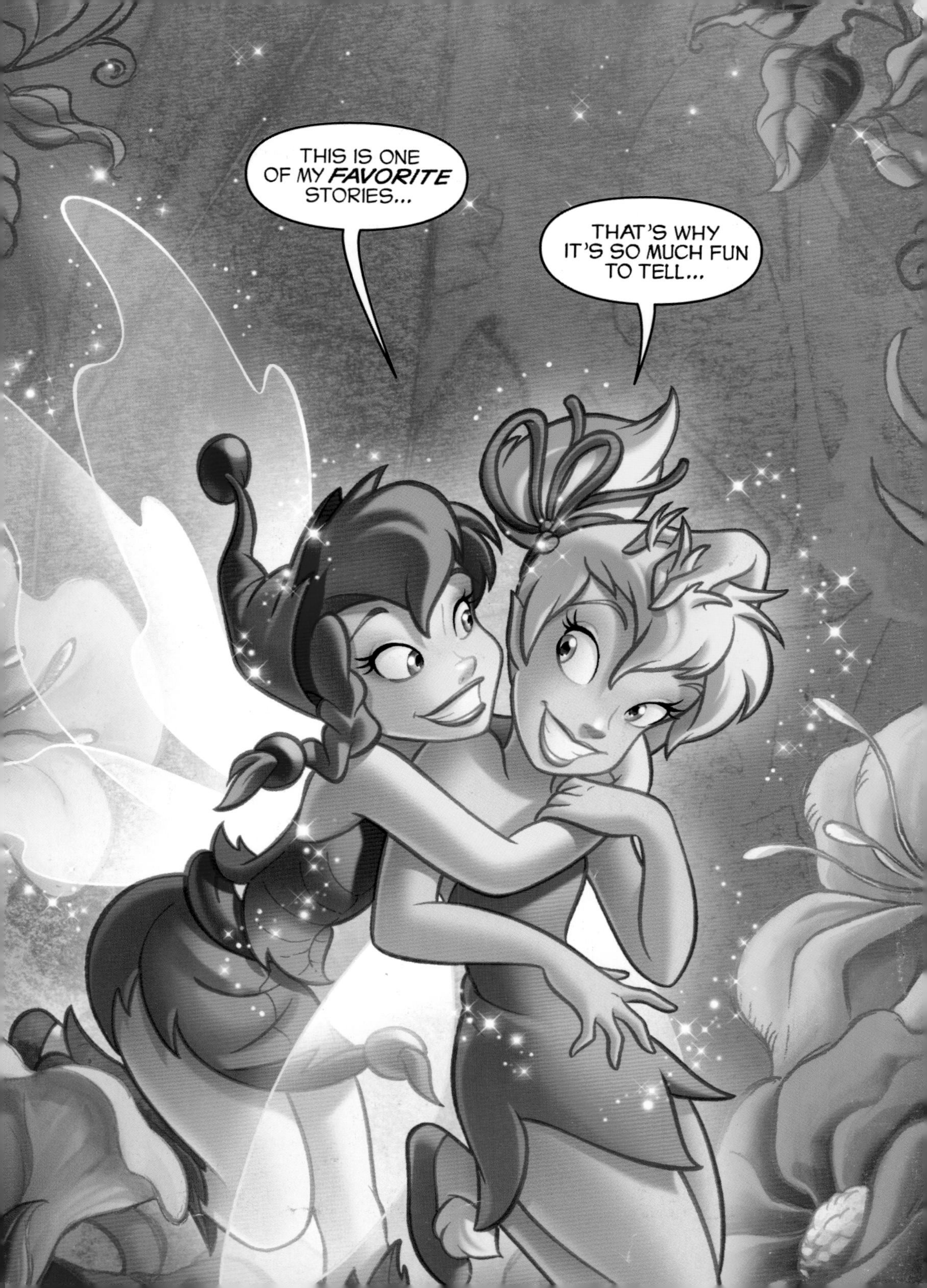
THIS IS ONE OF MY *FAVORITE* STORIES...
THAT'S WHY IT'S SO MUCH FUN TO TELL...

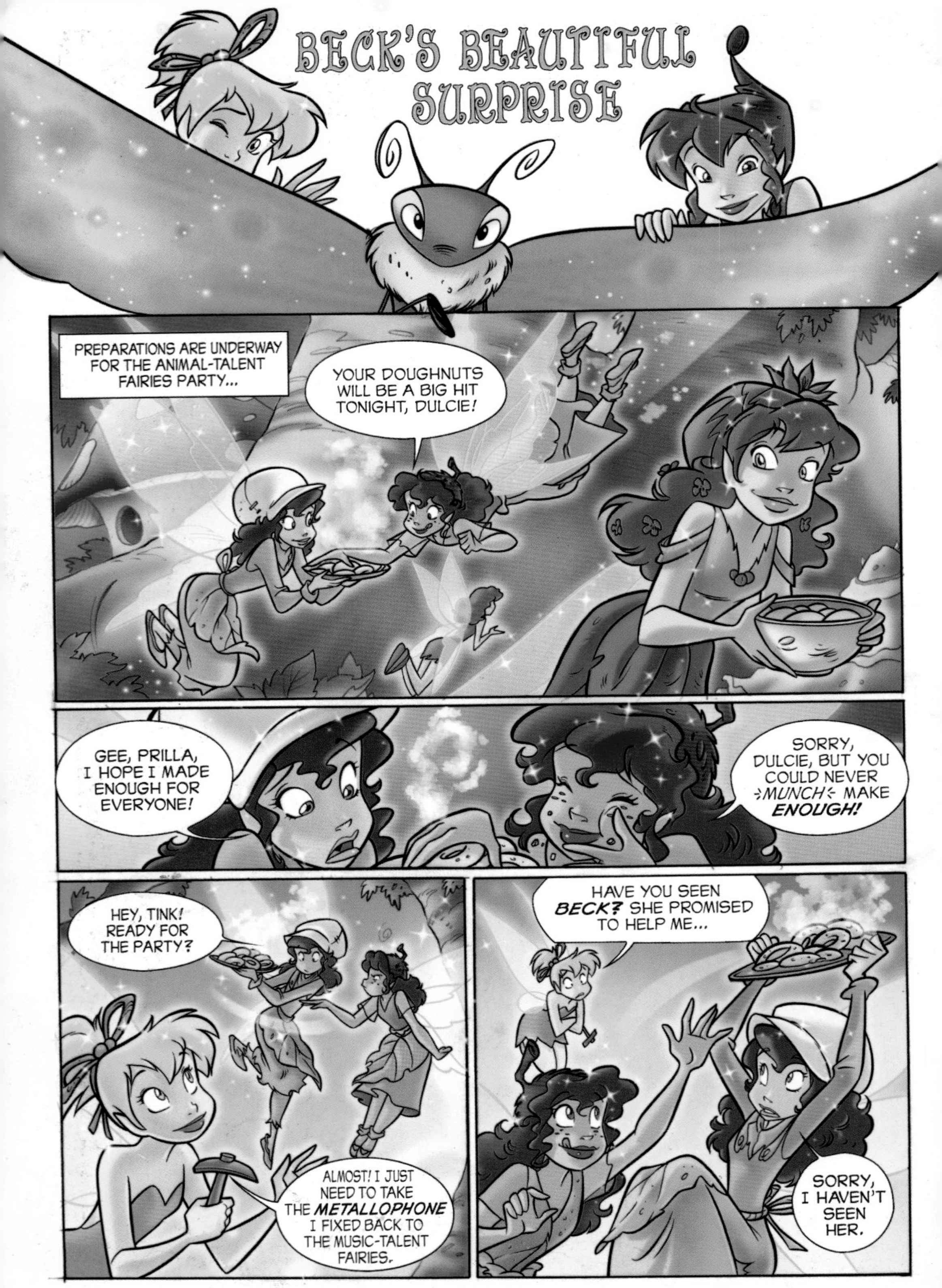
BECK'S BEAUTIFUL SURPRISE
PREPARATIONS ARE UNDERWAY FOR THE ANIMAL-TALENT FAIRIES PARTY...
YOUR DOUGHNUTS WILL BE A BIG HIT TONIGHT, DULCIE!
GEE, PRILLA, I HOPE I MADE ENOUGH FOR EVERYONE!
SORRY, DULCIE, BUT YOU COULD NEVER *MUNCH* MAKE ENOUGH!
HEY, TINK! READY FOR THE PARTY?
ALMOST! I JUST NEED TO TAKE THE METALLOPHONE I FIXED BACK TO THE MUSIC-TALENT FAIRIES.
HAVE YOU SEEN BECK? SHE PROMISED TO HELP ME...
SORRY, I HAVEN'T SEEN HER.

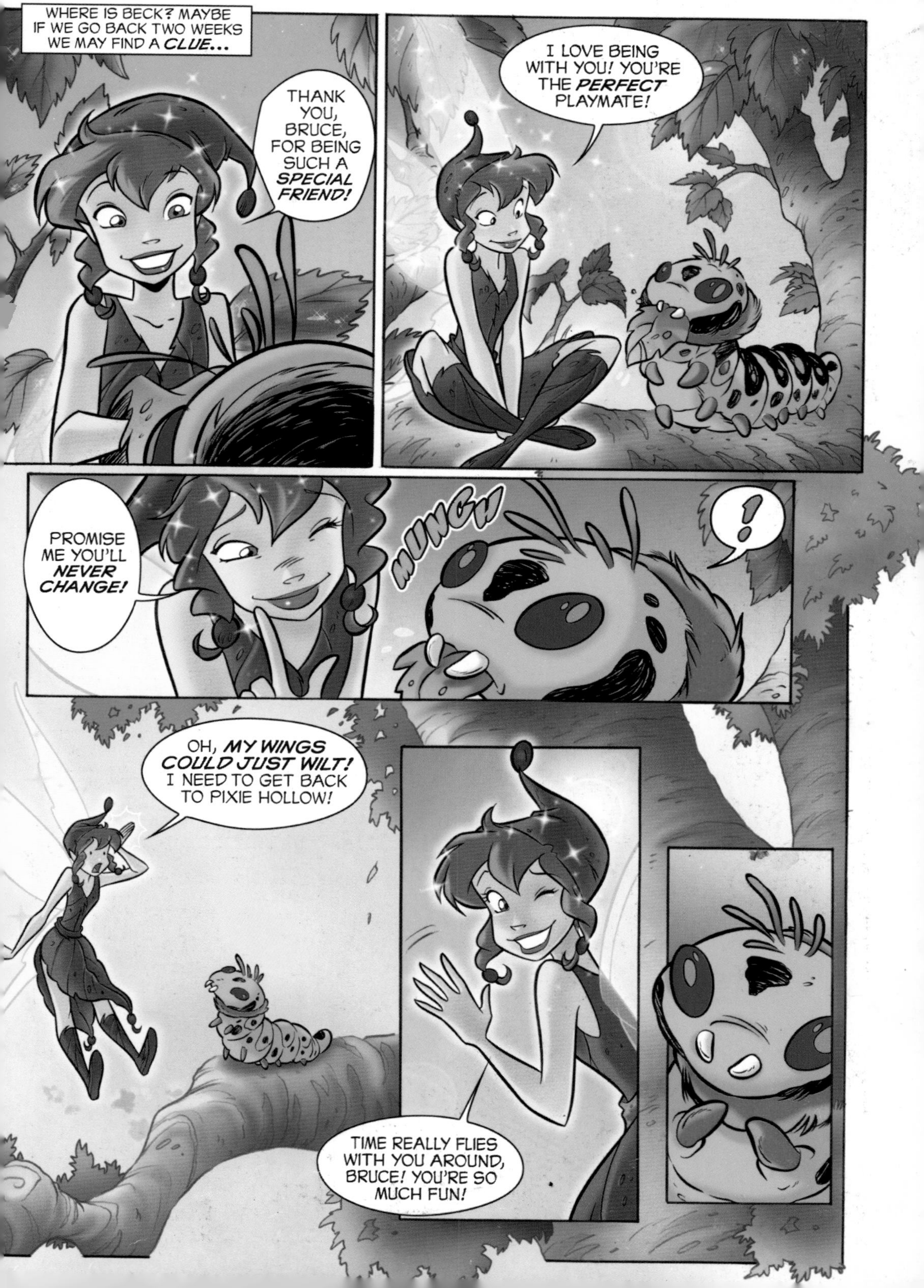

WHERE IS BECK? MAYBE IF WE GO BACK TWO WEEKS WE MAY FIND A CLUE...
THANK YOU, BRUCE, FOR BEING SUCH A SPECIAL FRIEND!
I LOVE BEING WITH YOU! YOU'RE THE PERFECT PLAYMATE!
PROMISE ME YOU'LL NEVER CHANGE!
MUNCH
!
OH, MY WINGS COULD JUST WILT! I NEED TO GET BACK TO PIXIE HOLLOW!
TIME REALLY FLIES WITH YOU AROUND, BRUCE! YOU'RE SO MUCH FUN!

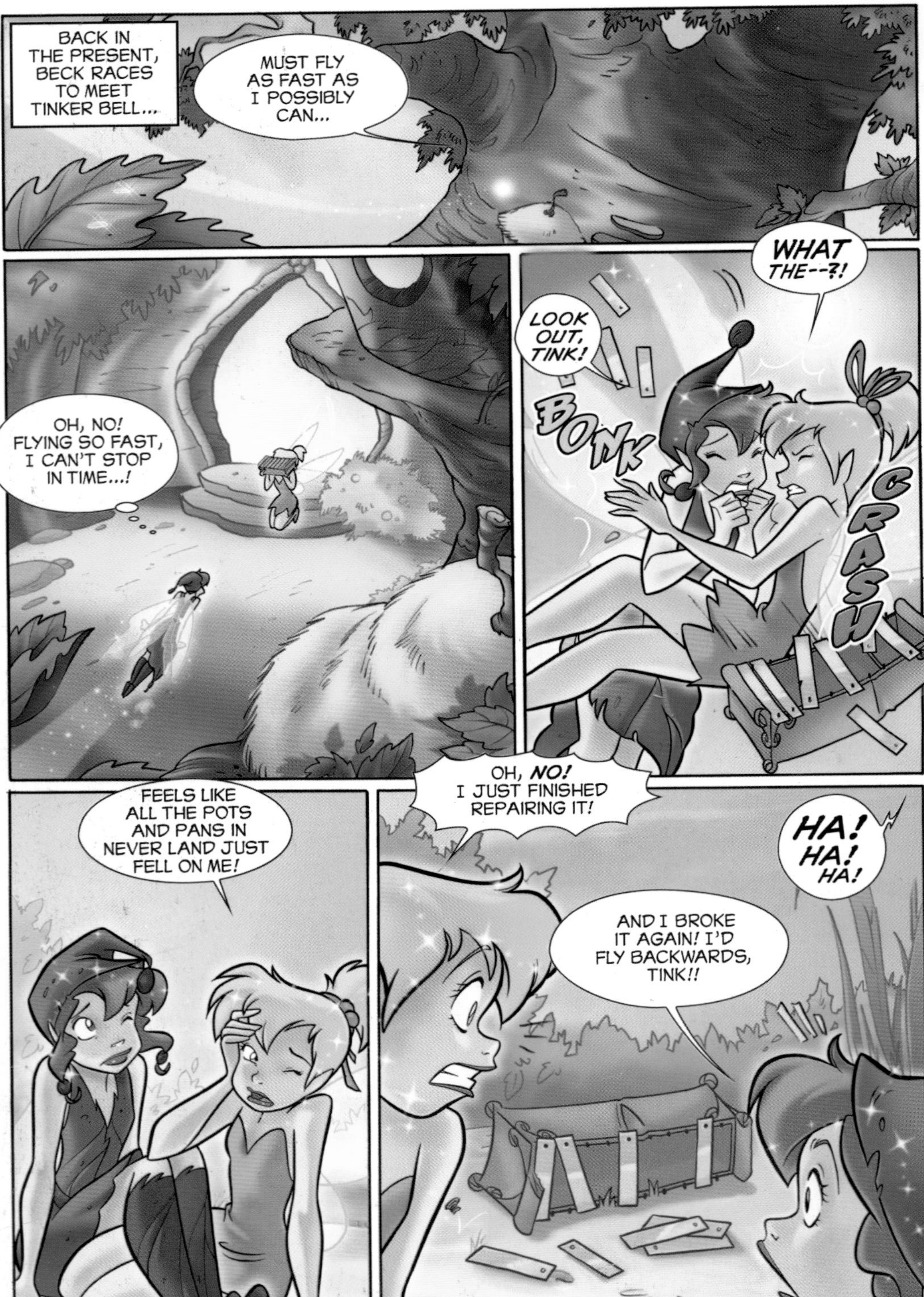

BACK IN THE PRESENT, BECK RACES TO MEET TINKER BELL...
MUST FLY AS FAST AS I POSSIBLY CAN...
OH, NO! FLYING SO FAST, I CAN'T STOP IN TIME...!
LOOK OUT, TINK!
WHAT THE--?!
BONK
CRASH
FEELS LIKE ALL THE POTS AND PANS IN NEVER LAND JUST FELL ON ME!
OH, NO! I JUST FINISHED REPAIRING IT!
HA! HA! HA!
AND I BROKE IT AGAIN! I'D FLY BACKWARDS, TINK!!

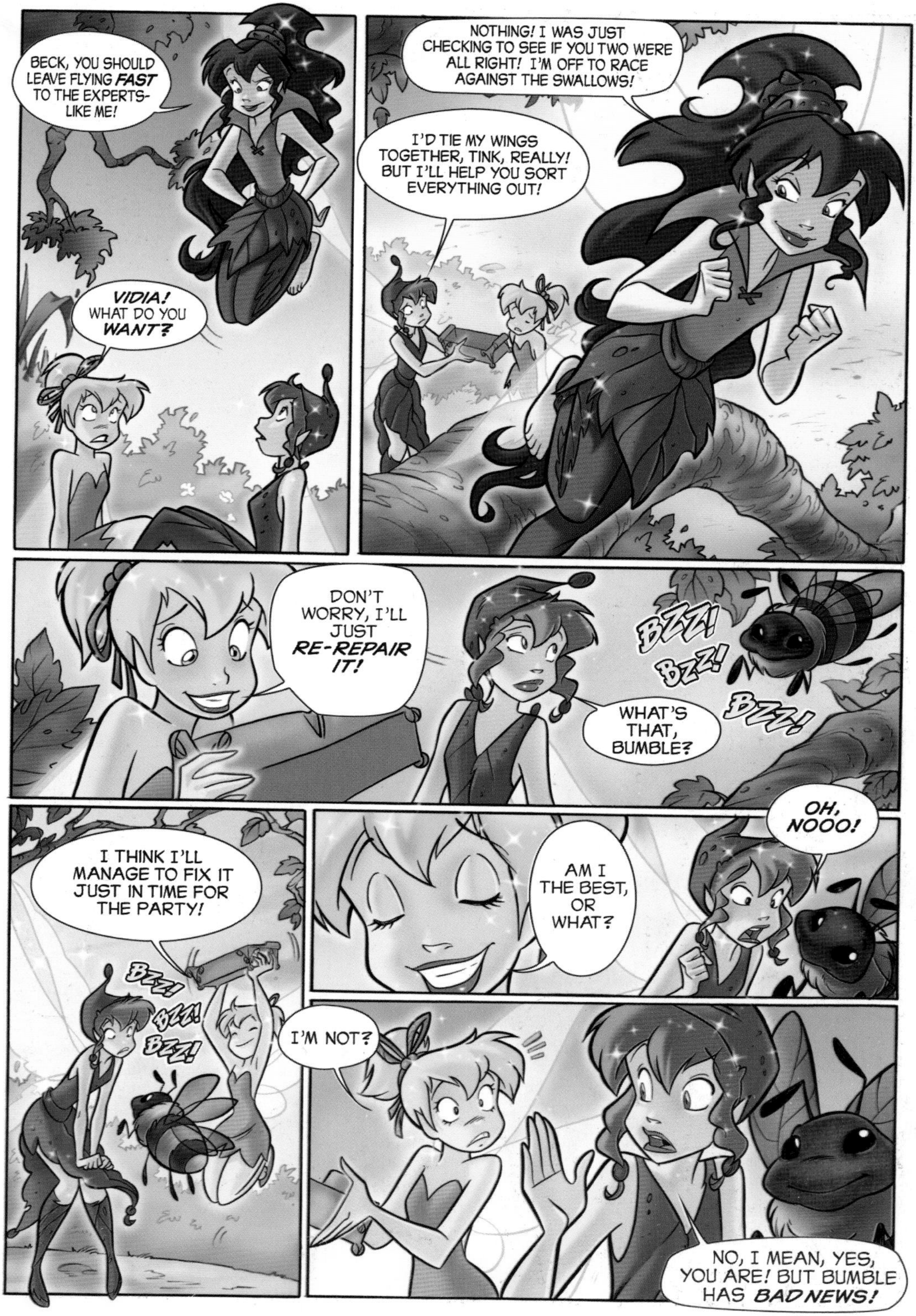

BECK, YOU SHOULD LEAVE FLYING FAST TO THE EXPERTS- LIKE ME!
VIDIA! WHAT DO YOU WANT?
NOTHING! I WAS JUST CHECKING TO SEE IF YOU TWO WERE ALL RIGHT! I'M OFF TO RACE AGAINST THE SWALLOWS!
I'D TIE MY WINGS TOGETHER, TINK, REALLY! BUT I'LL HELP YOU SORT EVERYTHING OUT!
DON'T WORRY, I'LL JUST RE-REPAIR IT!
WHAT'S THAT, BUMBLE?
BZZ! BZZ! BZZ!
I THINK I'LL MANAGE TO FIX IT JUST IN TIME FOR THE PARTY!
BZZ! BZZ! BZZ!
AM I THE BEST, OR WHAT?
OH, NOOO!
I'M NOT?
NO, I MEAN, YES, YOU ARE! BUT BUMBLE HAS BAD NEWS!

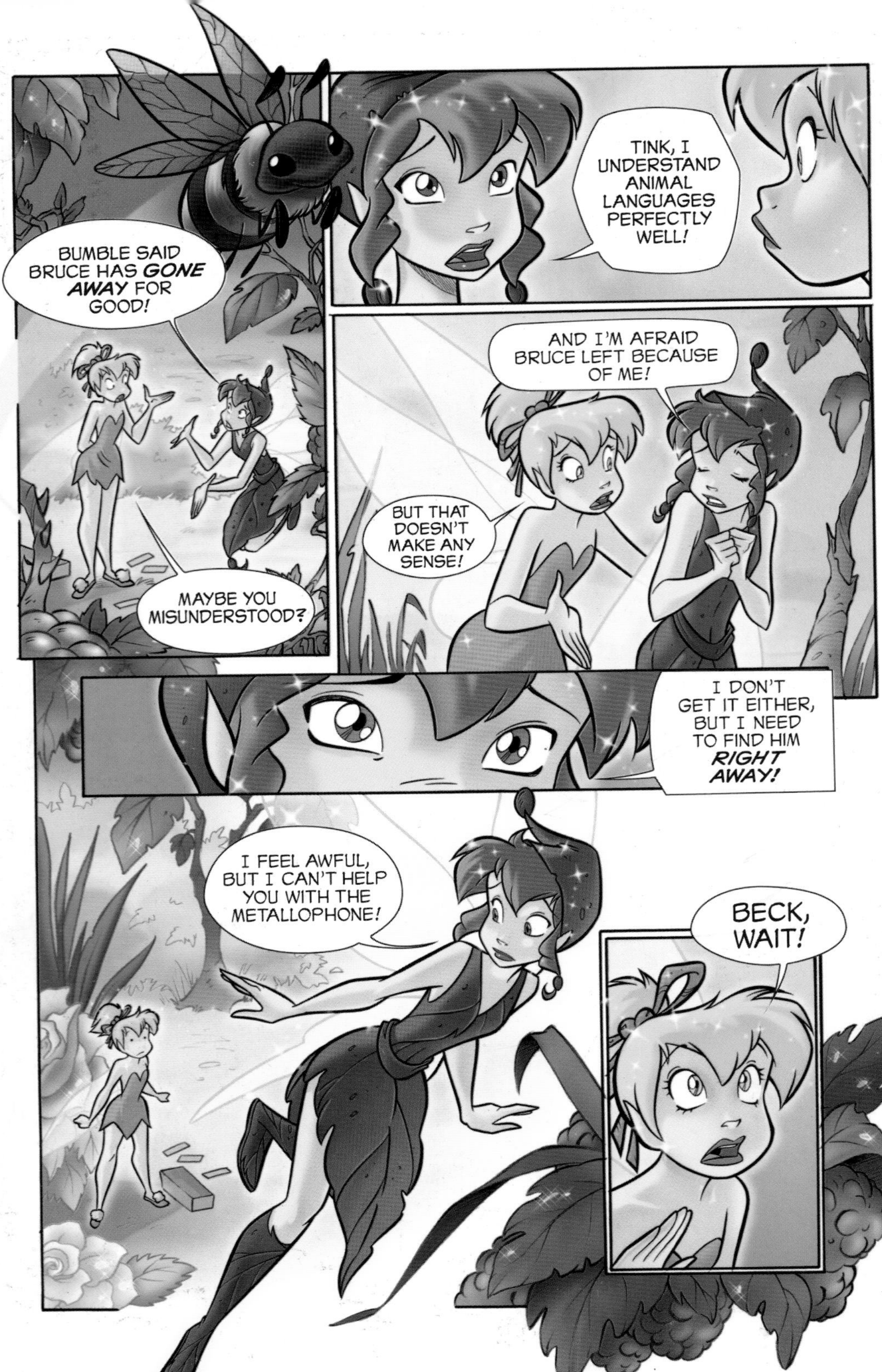
BUMBLE SAID BRUCE HAS GONE AWAY FOR GOOD!
MAYBE YOU MISUNDERSTOOD?
TINK, I UNDERSTAND ANIMAL LANGUAGES PERFECTLY WELL!
AND I'M AFRAID BRUCE LEFT BECAUSE OF ME!
BUT THAT DOESN'T MAKE ANY SENSE!
I DON'T GET IT EITHER, BUT I NEED TO FIND HIM RIGHT AWAY!
I FEEL AWFUL, BUT I CAN'T HELP YOU WITH THE METALLOPHONE!
BECK, WAIT!

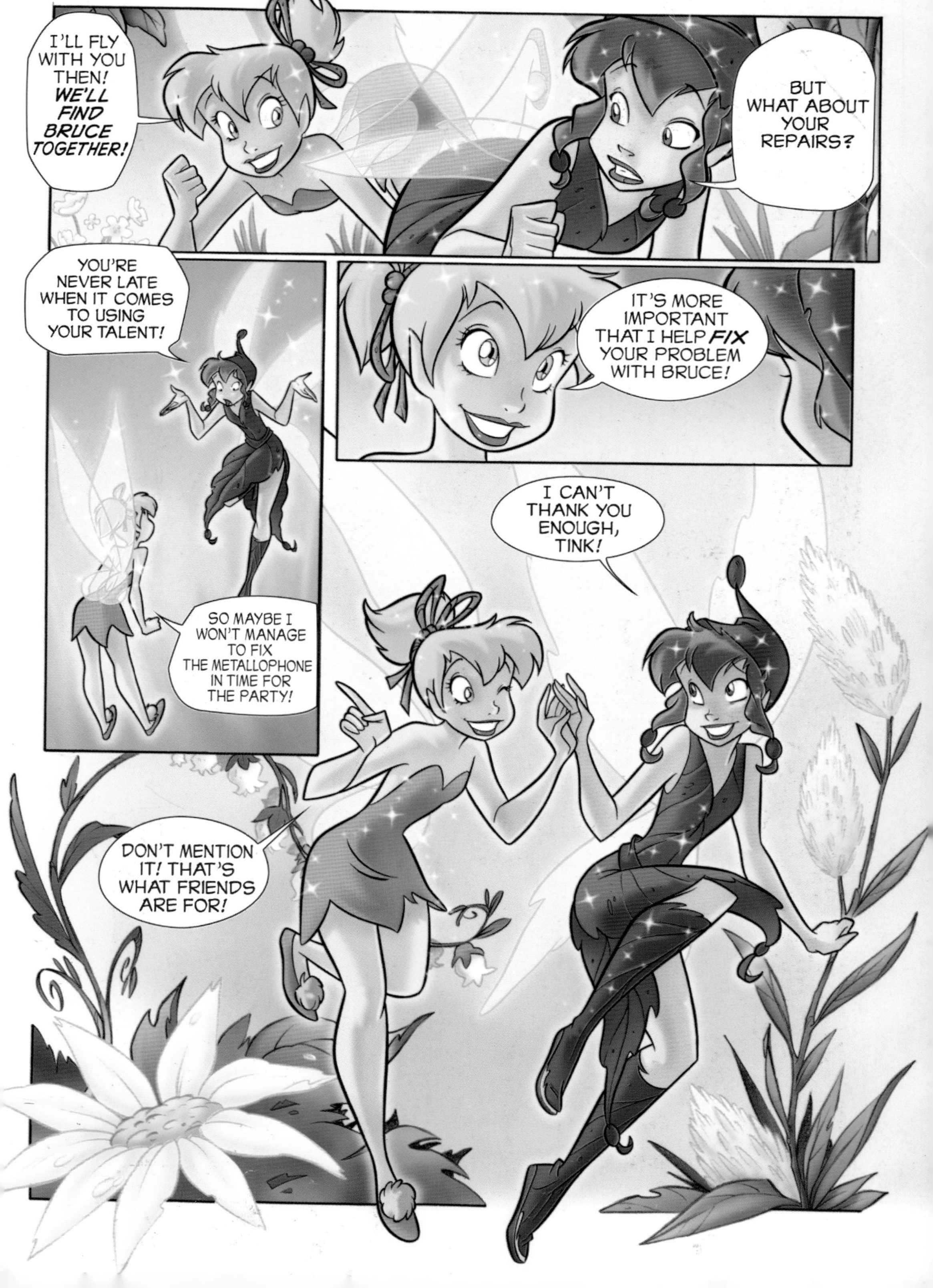
I'LL FLY WITH YOU THEN! ***WE'LL FIND BRUCE TOGETHER!***
BUT WHAT ABOUT YOUR REPAIRS?
YOU'RE NEVER LATE WHEN IT COMES TO USING YOUR TALENT!
IT'S MORE IMPORTANT THAT I HELP ***FIX*** YOUR PROBLEM WITH BRUCE!
SO MAYBE I WON'T MANAGE TO FIX THE METALLOPHONE IN TIME FOR THE PARTY!
I CAN'T THANK YOU ENOUGH, TINK!
DON'T MENTION IT! THAT'S WHAT FRIENDS ARE FOR!

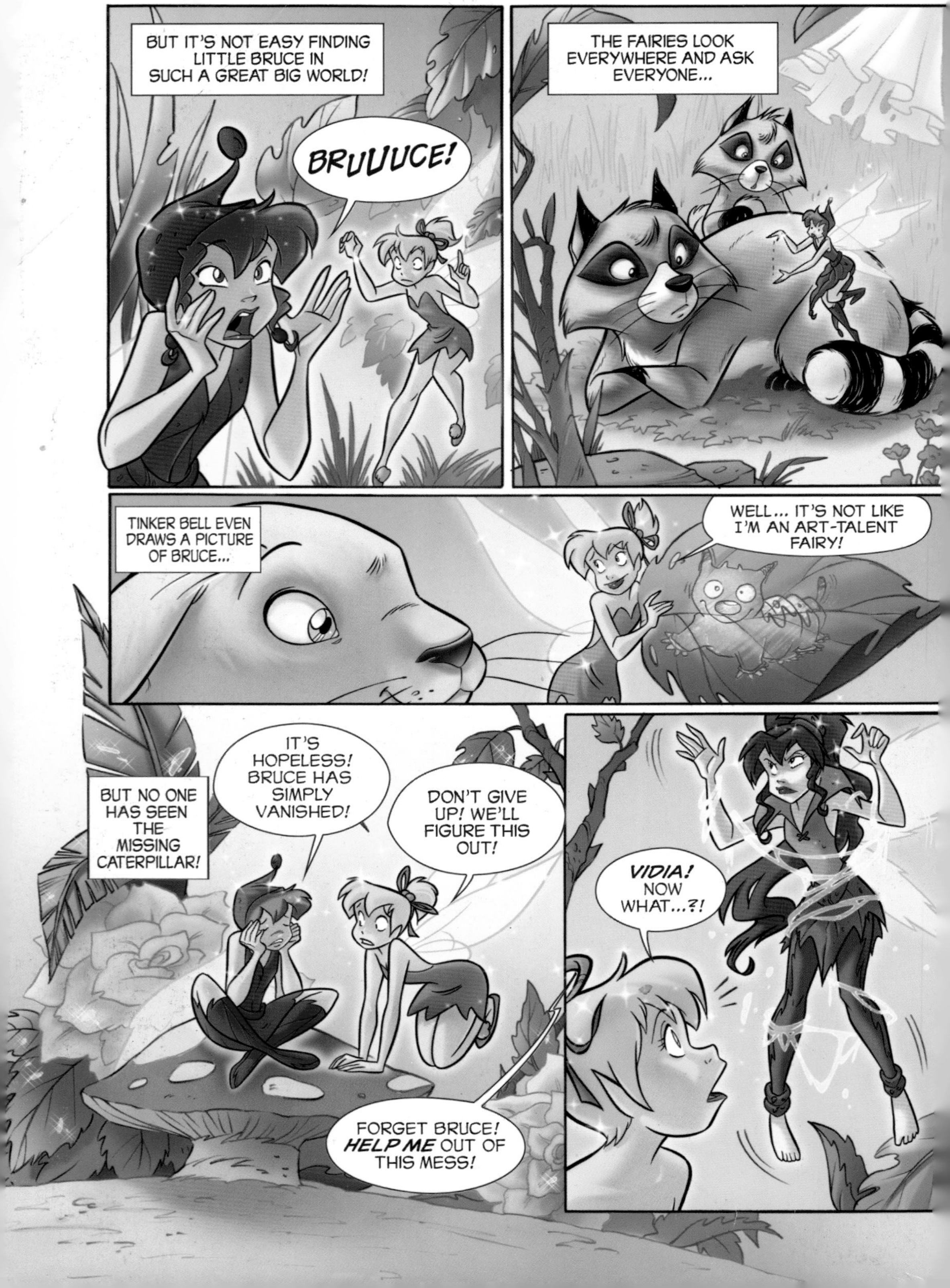
BUT IT'S NOT EASY FINDING LITTLE BRUCE IN SUCH A GREAT BIG WORLD!
BRUUUCE!
THE FAIRIES LOOK EVERYWHERE AND ASK EVERYONE...
TINKER BELL EVEN DRAWS A PICTURE OF BRUCE...
WELL... IT'S NOT LIKE I'M AN ART-TALENT FAIRY!
BUT NO ONE HAS SEEN THE MISSING CATERPILLAR!
IT'S HOPELESS! BRUCE HAS SIMPLY VANISHED!
DON'T GIVE UP! WE'LL FIGURE THIS OUT!
FORGET BRUCE! HELP ME OUT OF THIS MESS!
VIDIA! NOW WHAT...?!

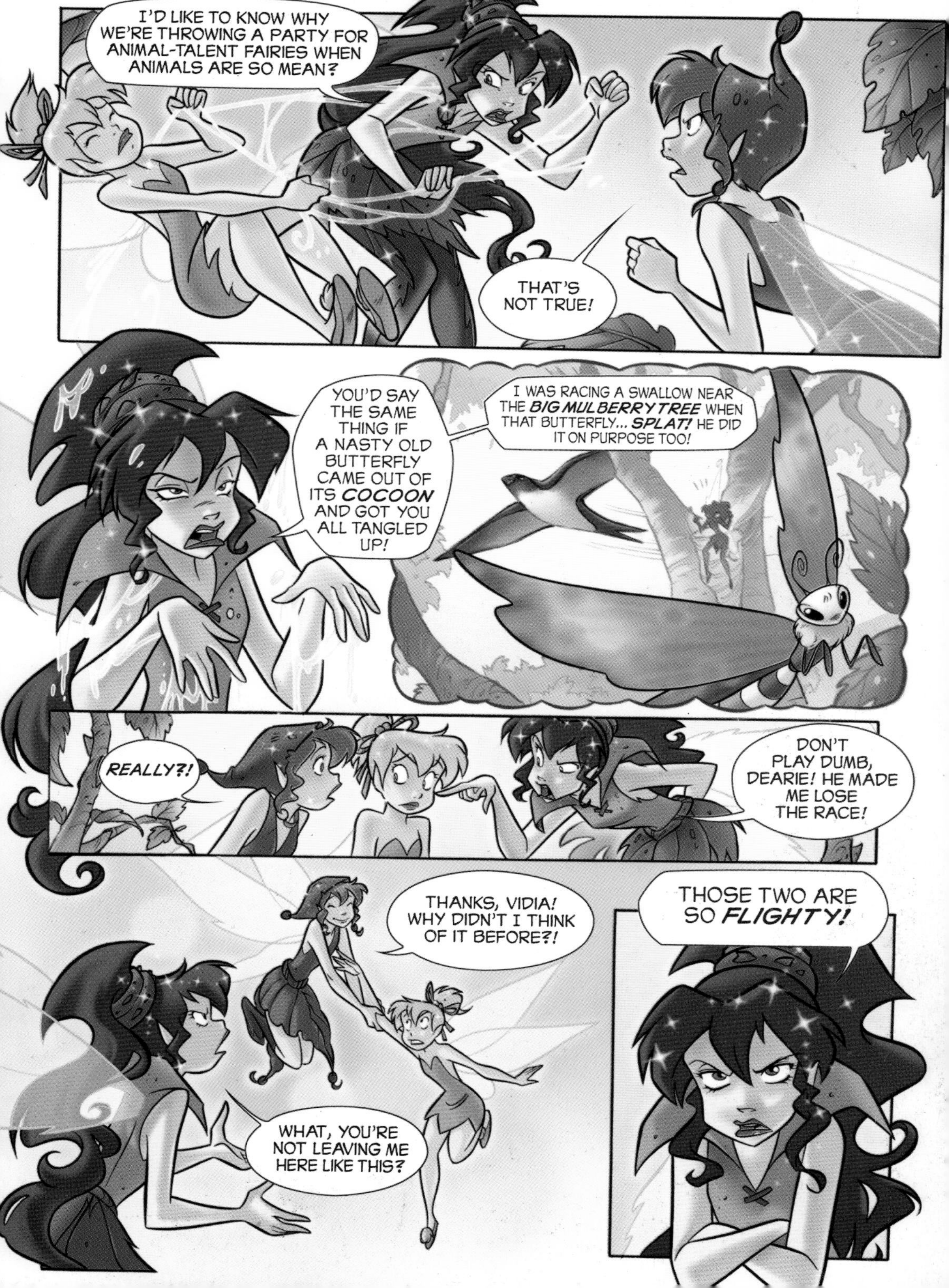

I'D LIKE TO KNOW WHY WE'RE THROWING A PARTY FOR ANIMAL-TALENT FAIRIES WHEN ANIMALS ARE SO MEAN?
THAT'S NOT TRUE!
YOU'D SAY THE SAME THING IF A NASTY OLD BUTTERFLY CAME OUT OF ITS COCOON AND GOT YOU ALL TANGLED UP!
I WAS RACING A SWALLOW NEAR THE BIG MULBERRY TREE WHEN THAT BUTTERFLY... SPLAT! HE DID IT ON PURPOSE TOO!
REALLY?!
DON'T PLAY DUMB, DEARIE! HE MADE ME LOSE THE RACE!
THANKS, VIDIA! WHY DIDN'T I THINK OF IT BEFORE?!
WHAT, YOU'RE NOT LEAVING ME HERE LIKE THIS?
THOSE TWO ARE SO FLIGHTY!

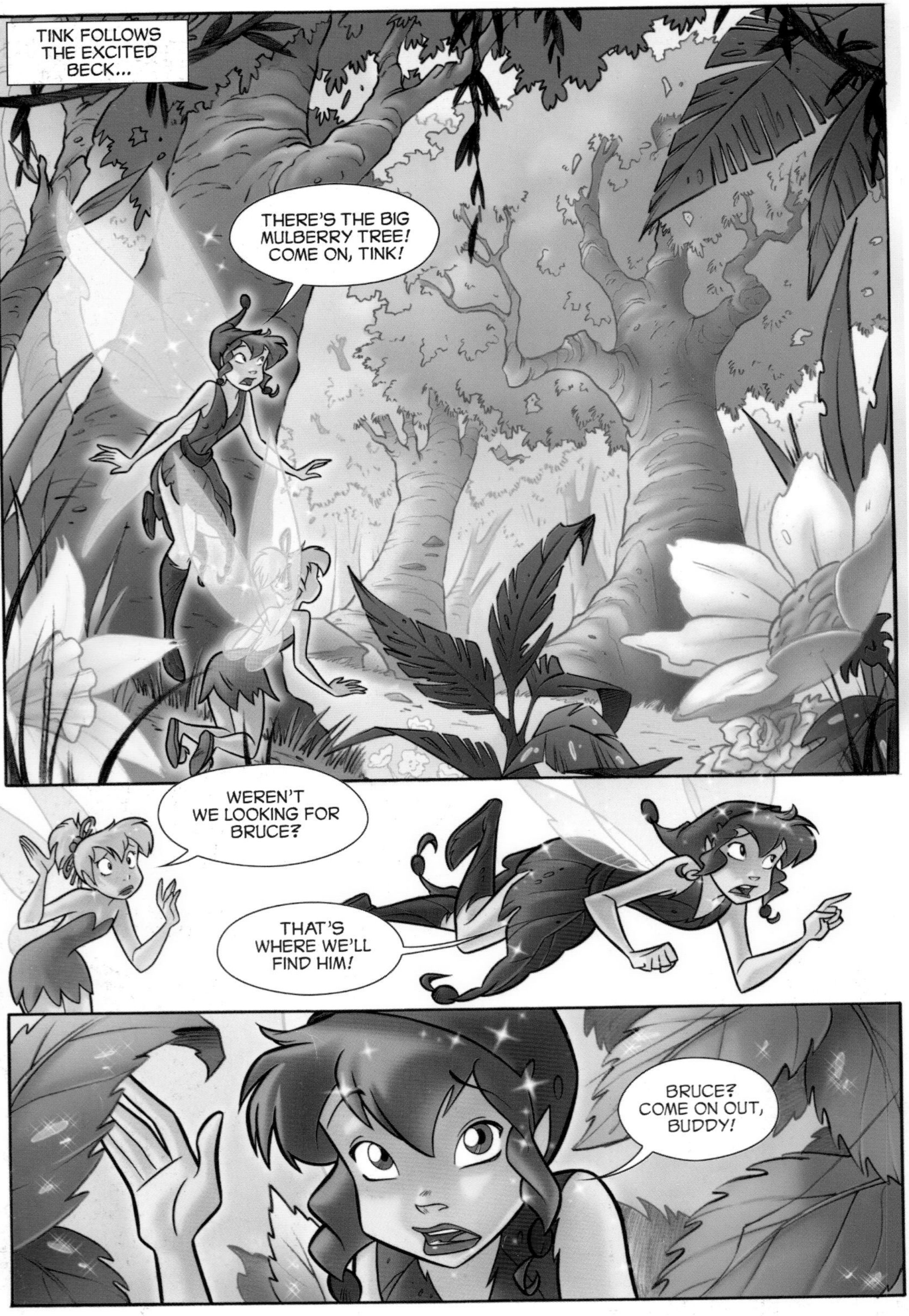
TINK FOLLOWS THE EXCITED BECK...
THERE'S THE BIG MULBERRY TREE! COME ON, TINK!
WEREN'T WE LOOKING FOR BRUCE?
THAT'S WHERE WE'LL FIND HIM!
BRUCE? COME ON OUT, BUDDY!

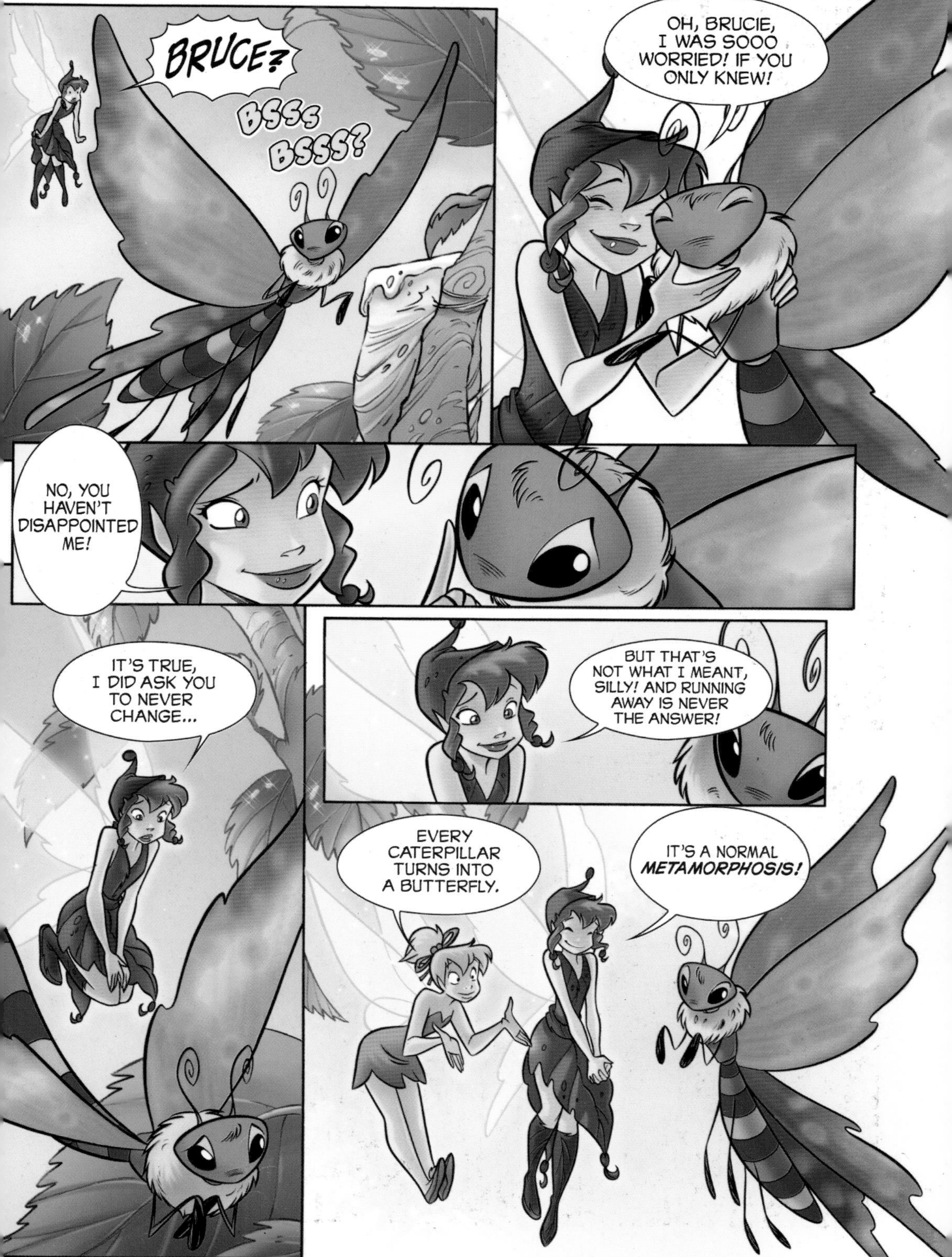
BRUCE?
BSSS BSSS?
OH, BRUCIE, I WAS SOOO WORRIED! IF YOU ONLY KNEW!
NO, YOU HAVEN'T DISAPPOINTED ME!
IT'S TRUE, I DID ASK YOU TO NEVER CHANGE...
BUT THAT'S NOT WHAT I MEANT, SILLY! AND RUNNING AWAY IS NEVER THE ANSWER!
EVERY CATERPILLAR TURNS INTO A BUTTERFLY.
IT'S A NORMAL *METAMORPHOSIS!*

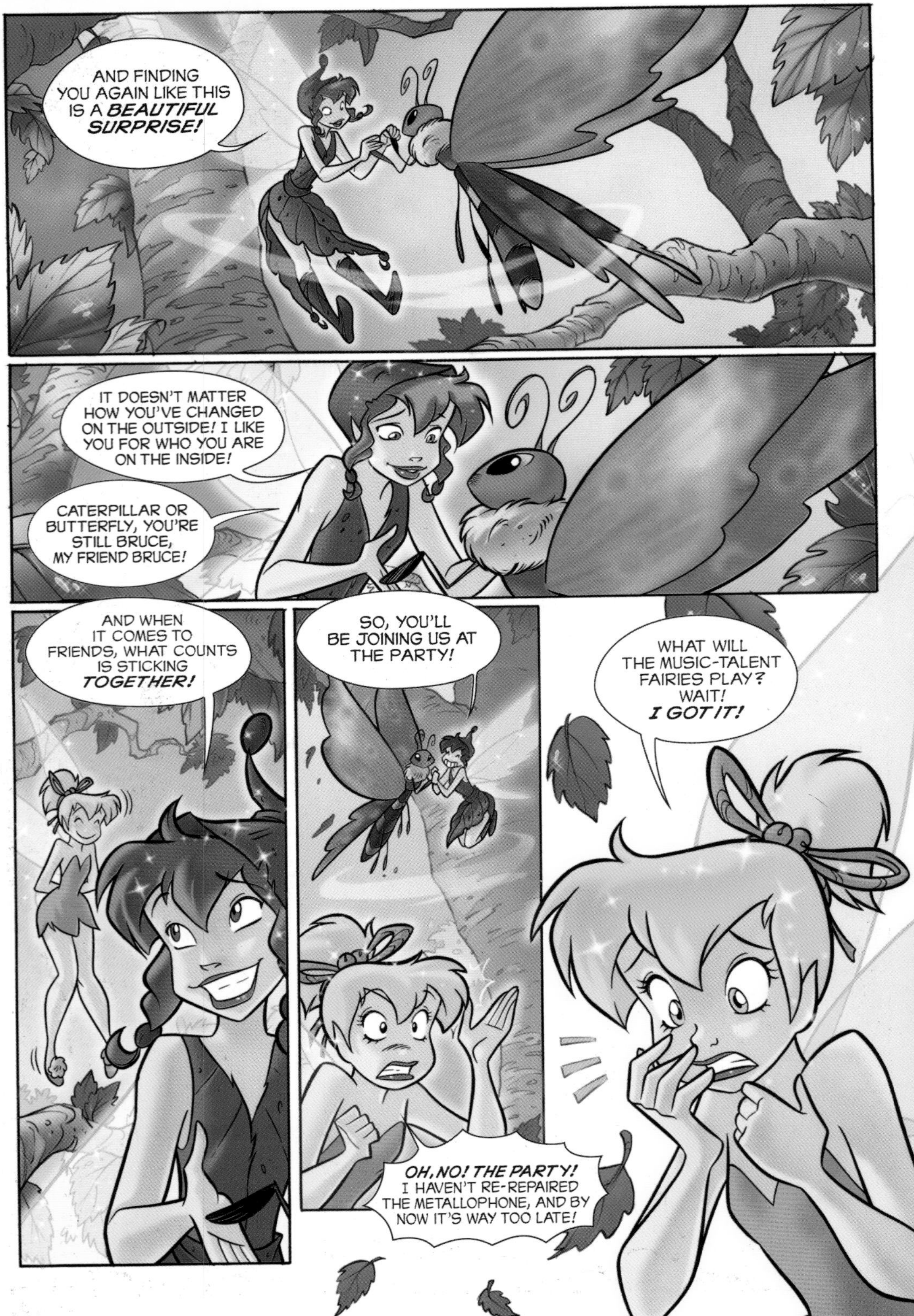
AND FINDING YOU AGAIN LIKE THIS IS A *BEAUTIFUL SURPRISE!*
IT DOESN'T MATTER HOW YOU'VE CHANGED ON THE OUTSIDE! I LIKE YOU FOR WHO YOU ARE ON THE INSIDE!
CATERPILLAR OR BUTTERFLY, YOU'RE STILL BRUCE, MY FRIEND BRUCE!
AND WHEN IT COMES TO FRIENDS, WHAT COUNTS IS STICKING *TOGETHER!*
SO, YOU'LL BE JOINING US AT THE PARTY!
WHAT WILL THE MUSIC-TALENT FAIRIES PLAY? WAIT! *I GOT IT!*
OH, NO! THE PARTY! I HAVEN'T RE-REPAIRED THE METALLOPHONE, AND BY NOW IT'S WAY TOO LATE!

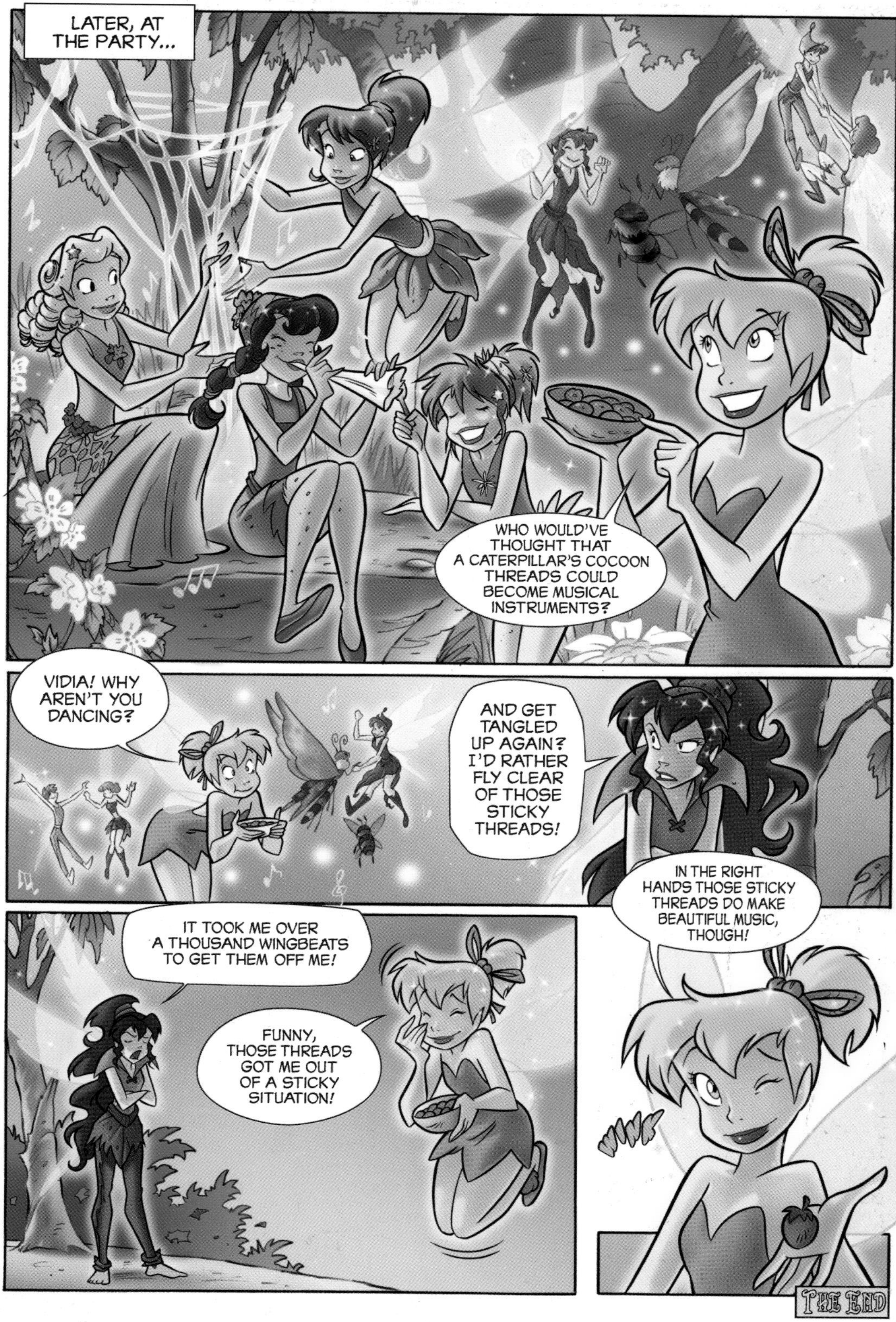
LATER, AT THE PARTY...
WHO WOULD'VE THOUGHT THAT A CATERPILLAR'S COCOON THREADS COULD BECOME MUSICAL INSTRUMENTS?
VIDIA! WHY AREN'T YOU DANCING?
AND GET TANGLED UP AGAIN? I'D RATHER FLY CLEAR OF THOSE STICKY THREADS!
IT TOOK ME OVER A THOUSAND WINGBEATS TO GET THEM OFF ME!
FUNNY, THOSE THREADS GOT ME OUT OF A STICKY SITUATION!
IN THE RIGHT HANDS THOSE STICKY THREADS DO MAKE BEAUTIFUL MUSIC, THOUGH!
THE END

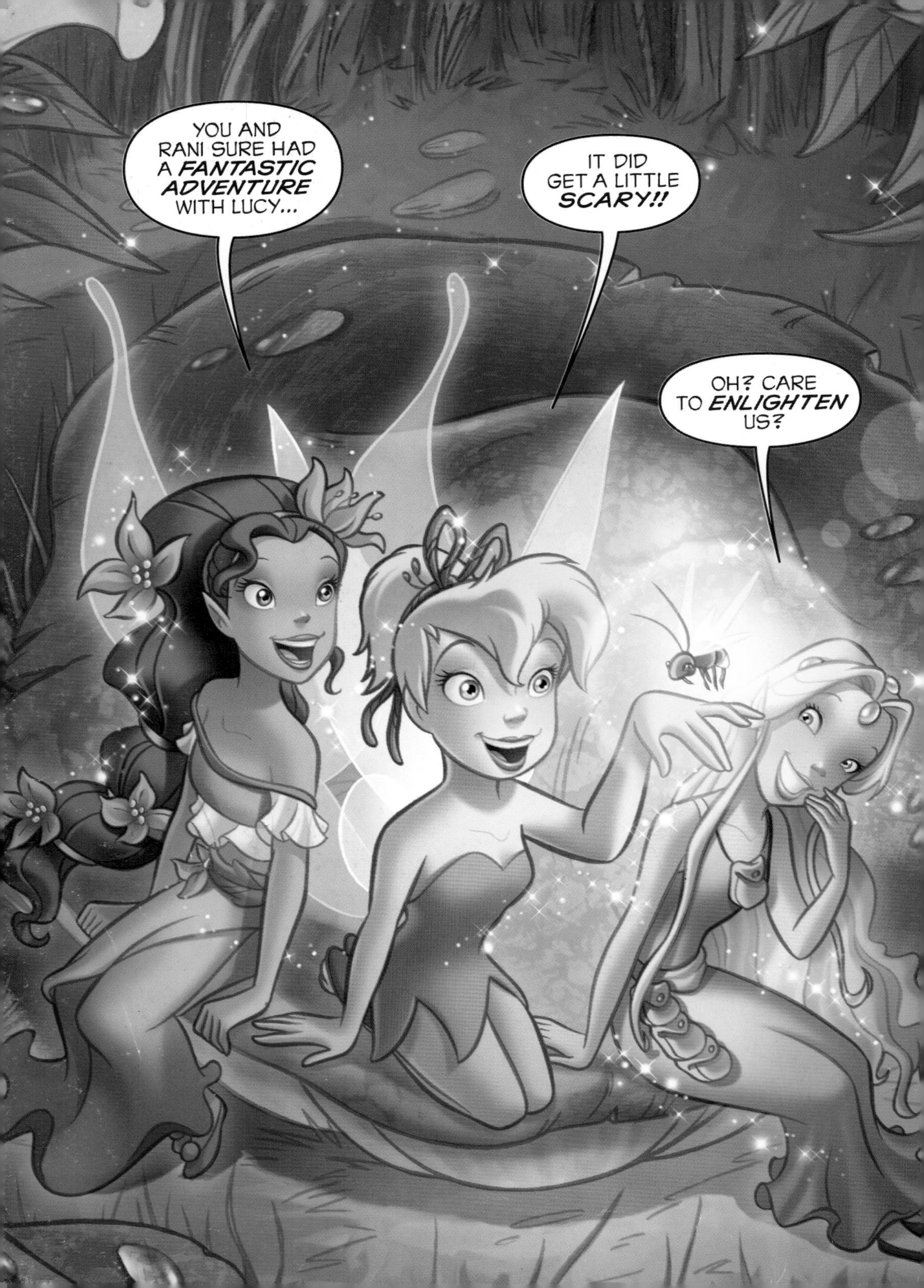
YOU AND RANI SURE HAD A *FANTASTIC ADVENTURE* WITH LUCY...
IT DID GET A LITTLE *SCARY!!*
OH? CARE TO *ENLIGHTEN* US?

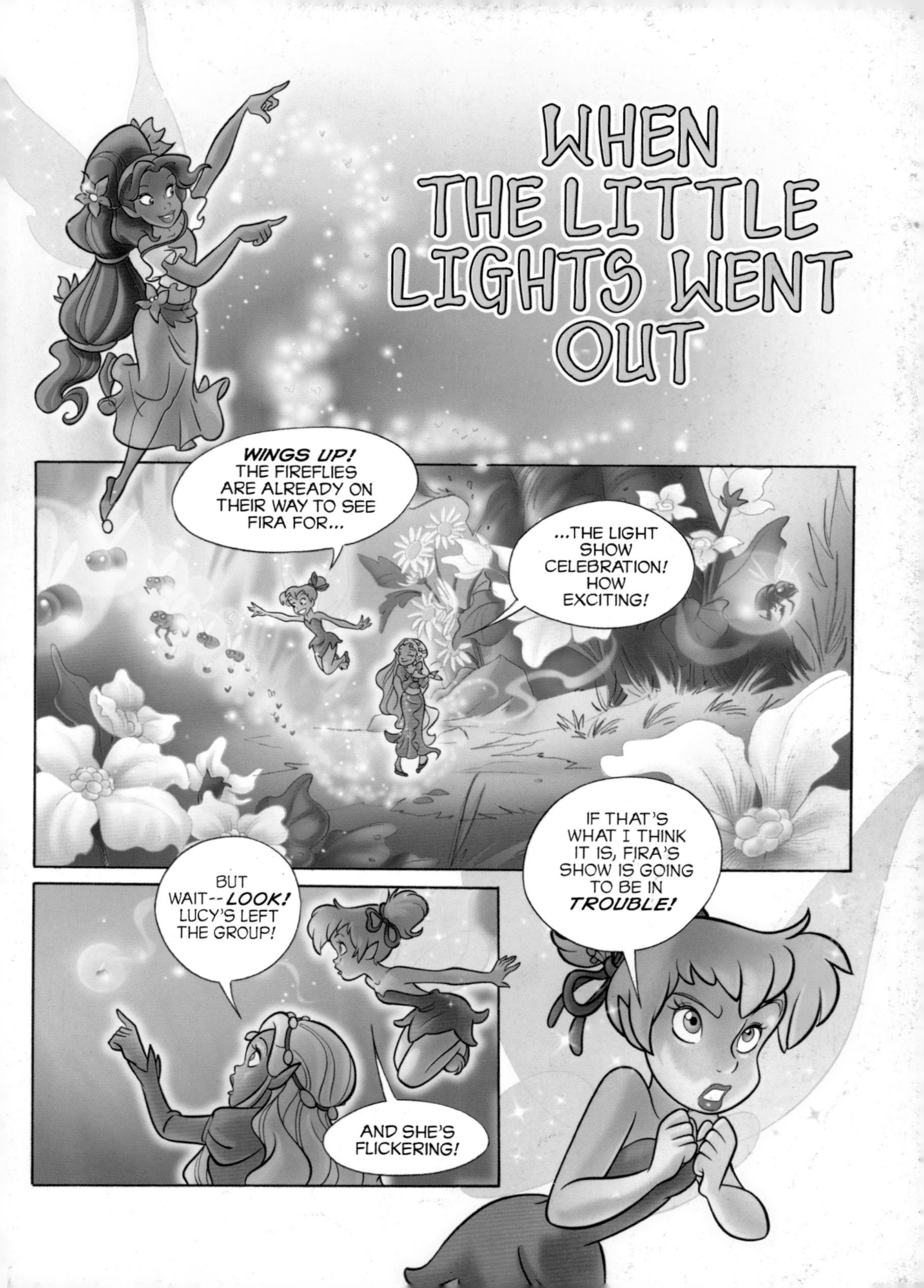
WHEN THE LITTLE LIGHTS WENT OUT
WINGS UP! THE FIREFLIES ARE ALREADY ON THEIR WAY TO SEE FIRA FOR...
...THE LIGHT SHOW CELEBRATION! HOW EXCITING!
BUT WAIT--LOOK! LUCY'S LEFT THE GROUP!
AND SHE'S FLICKERING!
IF THAT'S WHAT I THINK IT IS, FIRA'S SHOW IS GOING TO BE IN TROUBLE!

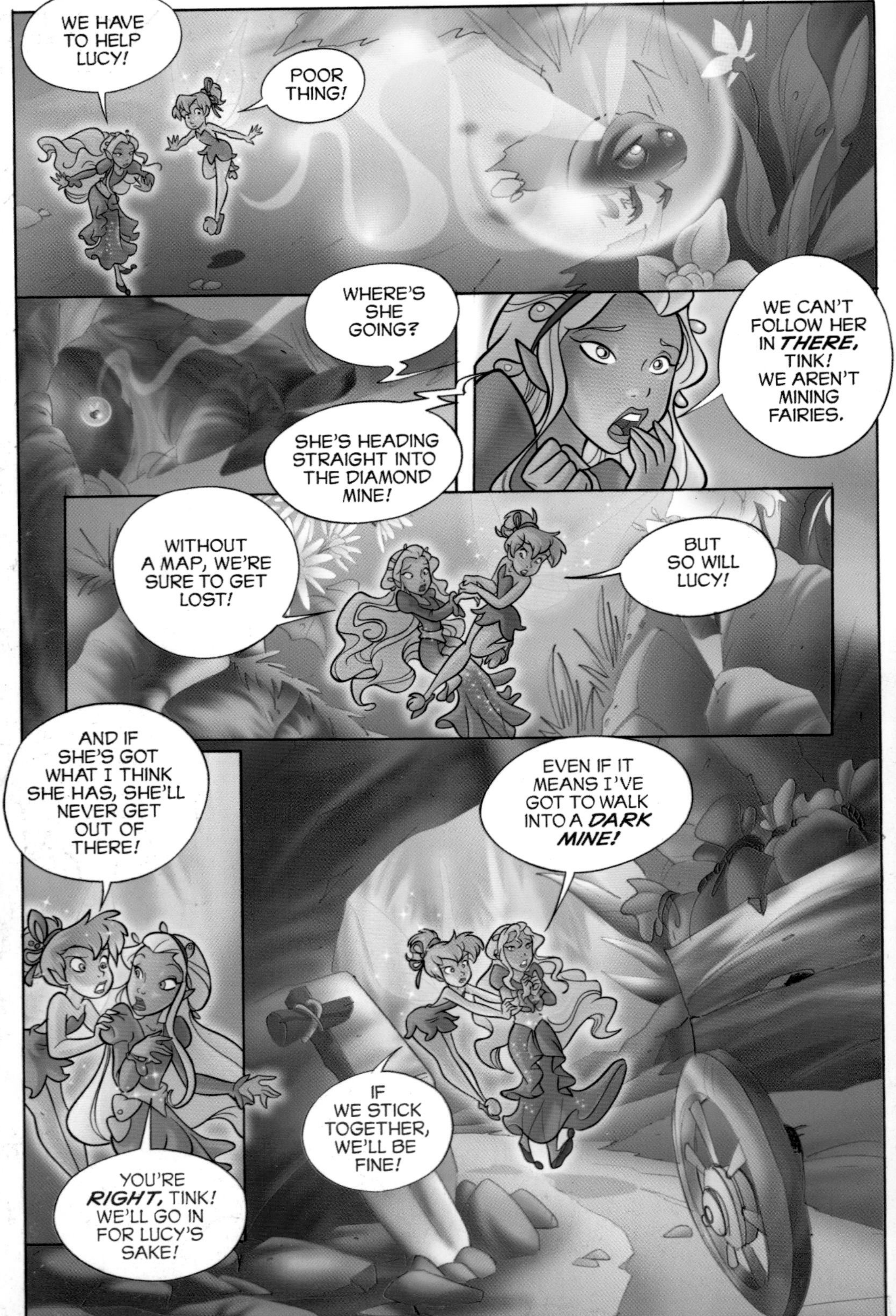
WE HAVE TO HELP LUCY!
POOR THING!
WHERE'S SHE GOING?
SHE'S HEADING STRAIGHT INTO THE DIAMOND MINE!
WE CAN'T FOLLOW HER IN THERE, TINK! WE AREN'T MINING FAIRIES.
WITHOUT A MAP, WE'RE SURE TO GET LOST!
BUT SO WILL LUCY!
AND IF SHE'S GOT WHAT I THINK SHE HAS, SHE'LL NEVER GET OUT OF THERE!
EVEN IF IT MEANS I'VE GOT TO WALK INTO A DARK MINE!
IF WE STICK TOGETHER, WE'LL BE FINE!
YOU'RE RIGHT, TINK! WE'LL GO IN FOR LUCY'S SAKE!

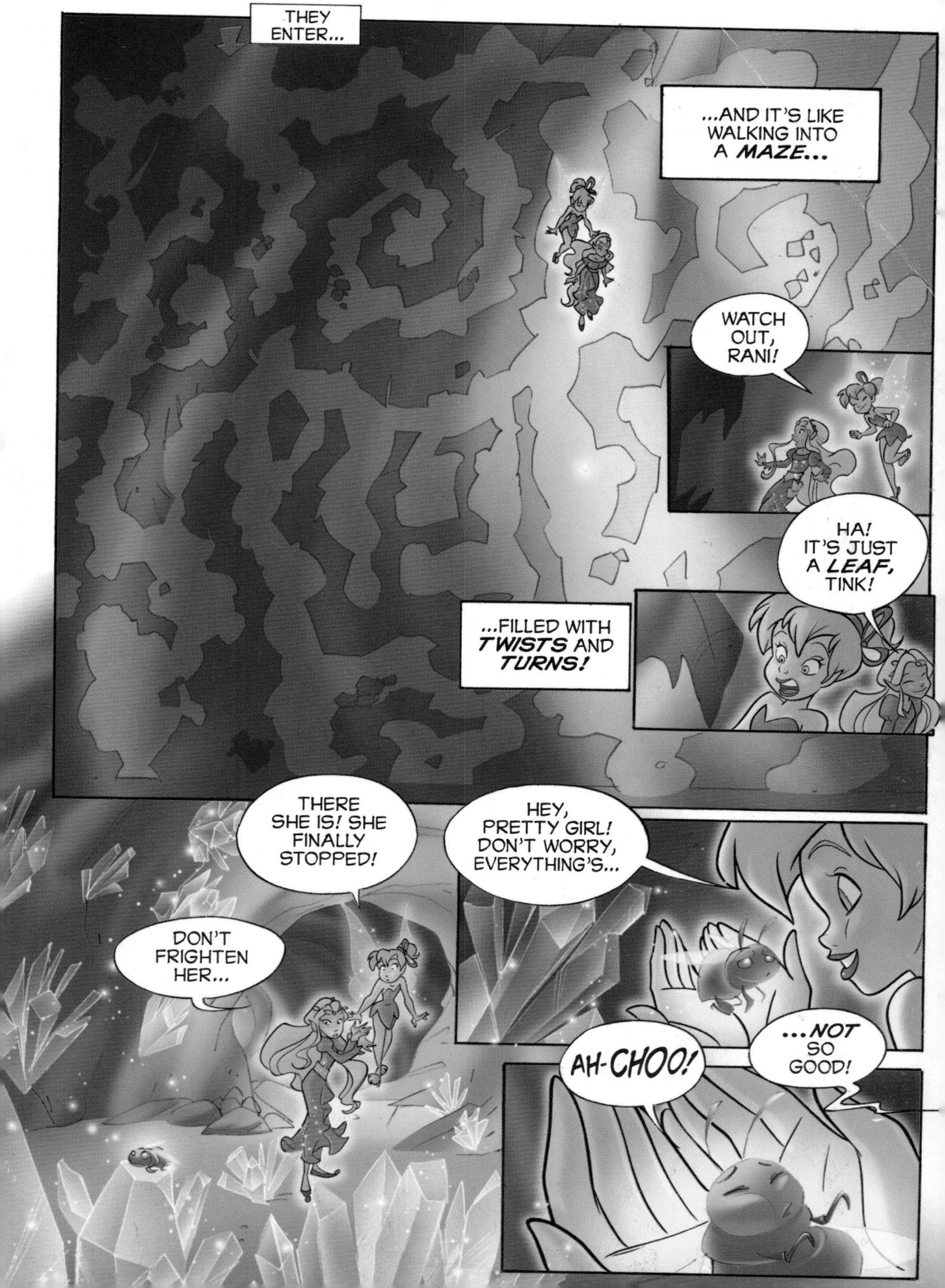
THEY ENTER...
...AND IT'S LIKE WALKING INTO A MAZE...
WATCH OUT, RANI!
...FILLED WITH TWISTS AND TURNS!
HA! IT'S JUST A LEAF, TINK!
THERE SHE IS! SHE FINALLY STOPPED!
DON'T FRIGHTEN HER...
HEY, PRETTY GIRL! DON'T WORRY, EVERYTHING'S...
AH-CHOO!
...NOT SO GOOD!

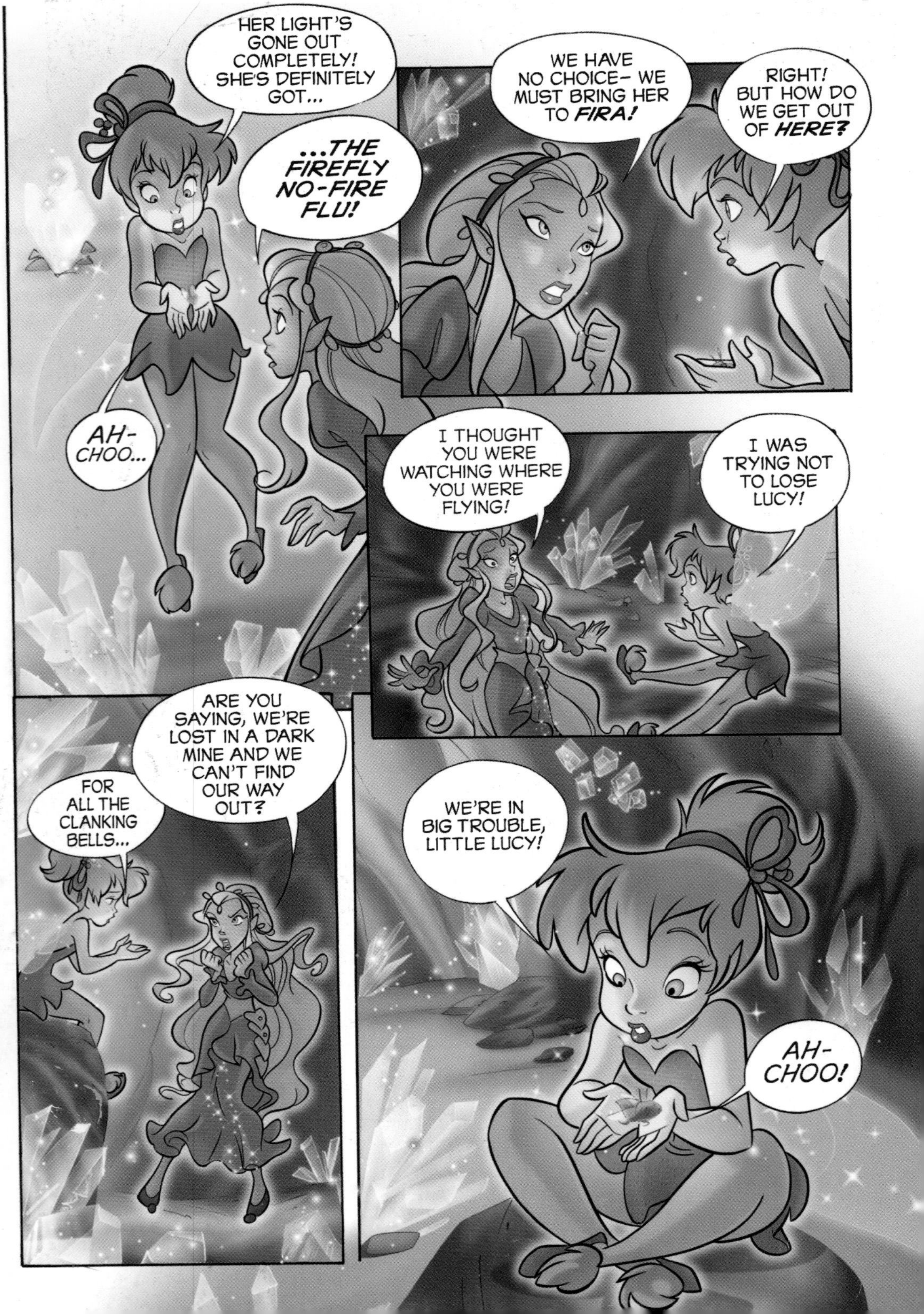
HER LIGHT'S GONE OUT COMPLETELY! SHE'S DEFINITELY GOT...
...THE FIREFLY NO-FIRE FLU!
AH-CHOO...
WE HAVE NO CHOICE– WE MUST BRING HER TO FIRA!
RIGHT! BUT HOW DO WE GET OUT OF HERE?
I THOUGHT YOU WERE WATCHING WHERE YOU WERE FLYING!
I WAS TRYING NOT TO LOSE LUCY!
ARE YOU SAYING, WE'RE LOST IN A DARK MINE AND WE CAN'T FIND OUR WAY OUT?
FOR ALL THE CLANKING BELLS...
WE'RE IN BIG TROUBLE, LITTLE LUCY!
AH-CHOO!

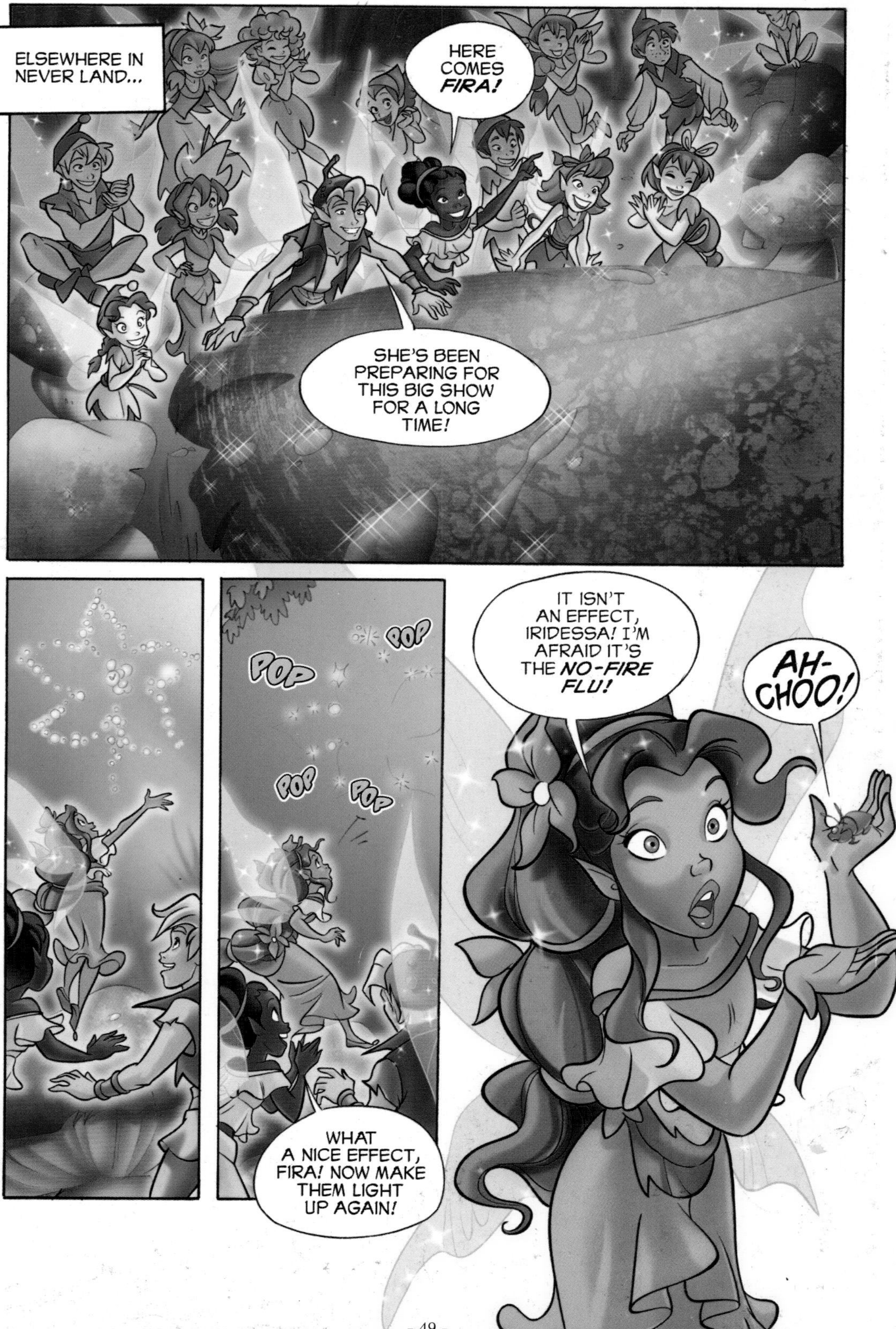
ELSEWHERE IN NEVER LAND...
HERE COMES *FIRA!*
SHE'S BEEN PREPARING FOR THIS BIG SHOW FOR A LONG TIME!
POP
POP
POP
POP
WHAT A NICE EFFECT, FIRA! NOW MAKE THEM LIGHT UP AGAIN!
IT ISN'T AN EFFECT, IRIDESSA! I'M AFRAID IT'S THE *NO-FIRE FLU!*
AH-CHOO!

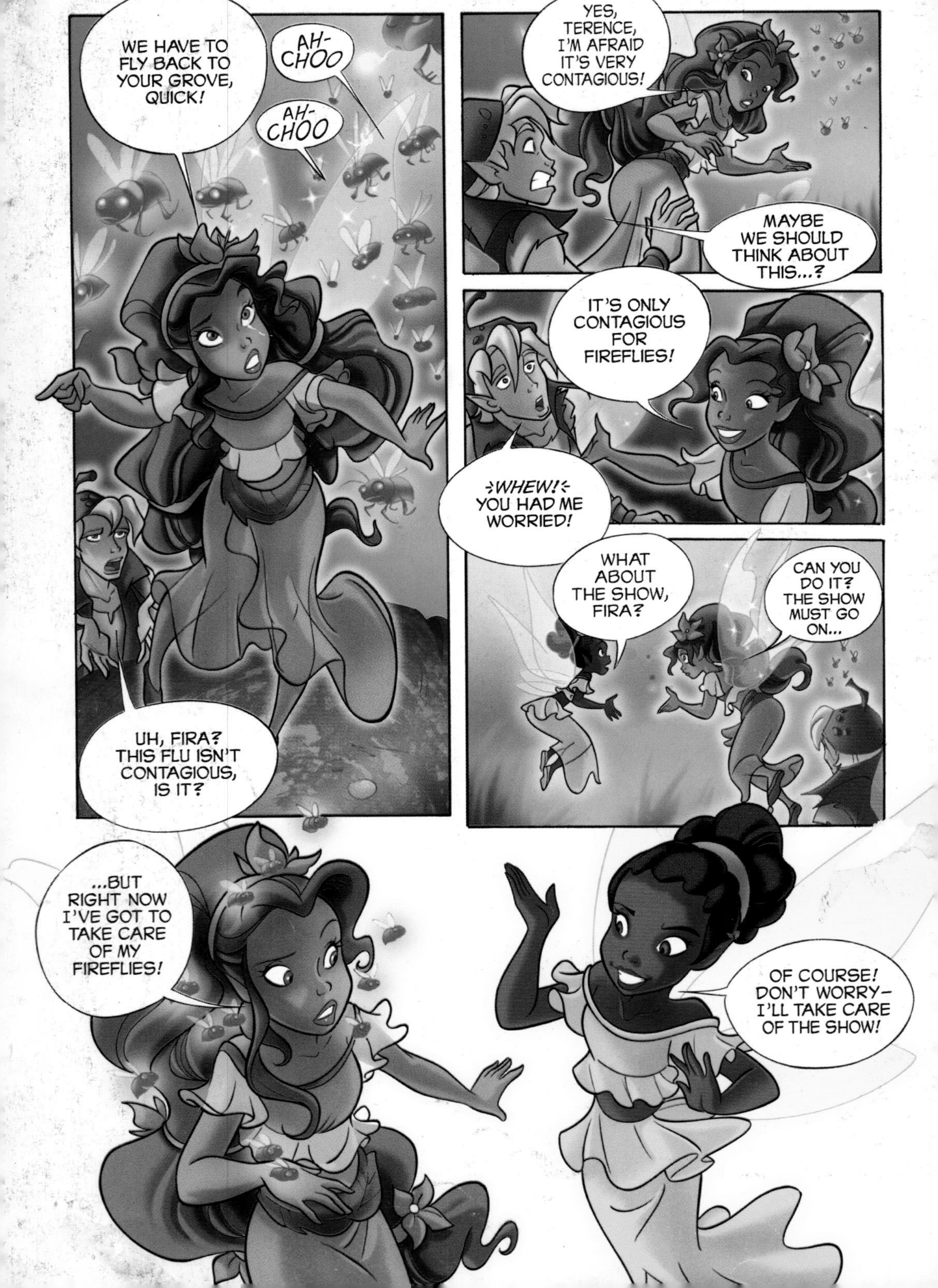
WE HAVE TO FLY BACK TO YOUR GROVE, QUICK!
AH-CHOO
AH-CHOO
UH, FIRA? THIS FLU ISN'T CONTAGIOUS, IS IT?
YES, TERENCE, I'M AFRAID IT'S VERY CONTAGIOUS!
MAYBE WE SHOULD THINK ABOUT THIS...?
IT'S ONLY CONTAGIOUS FOR FIREFLIES!
WHEW! YOU HAD ME WORRIED!
WHAT ABOUT THE SHOW, FIRA?
CAN YOU DO IT? THE SHOW MUST GO ON...
...BUT RIGHT NOW I'VE GOT TO TAKE CARE OF MY FIREFLIES!
OF COURSE! DON'T WORRY– I'LL TAKE CARE OF THE SHOW!

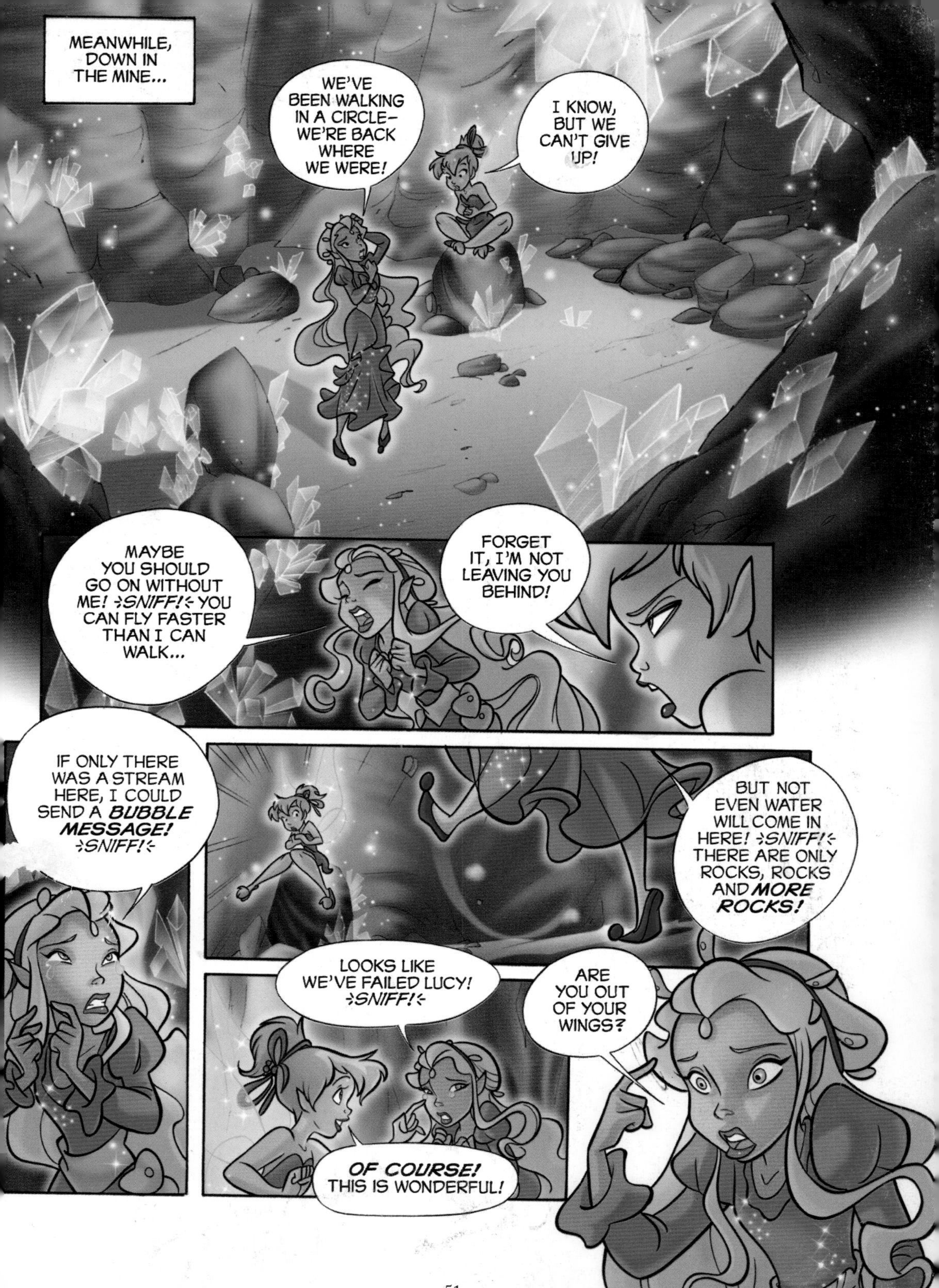

MEANWHILE, DOWN IN THE MINE...
WE'VE BEEN WALKING IN A CIRCLE– WE'RE BACK WHERE WE WERE!
I KNOW, BUT WE CAN'T GIVE UP!
MAYBE YOU SHOULD GO ON WITHOUT ME! *SNIFF!* YOU CAN FLY FASTER THAN I CAN WALK...
FORGET IT, I'M NOT LEAVING YOU BEHIND!
IF ONLY THERE WAS A STREAM HERE, I COULD SEND A BUBBLE MESSAGE! *SNIFF!*
BUT NOT EVEN WATER WILL COME IN HERE! *SNIFF!* THERE ARE ONLY ROCKS, ROCKS AND MORE ROCKS!
LOOKS LIKE WE'VE FAILED LUCY! *SNIFF!*
OF COURSE! THIS IS WONDERFUL!
ARE YOU OUT OF YOUR WINGS?

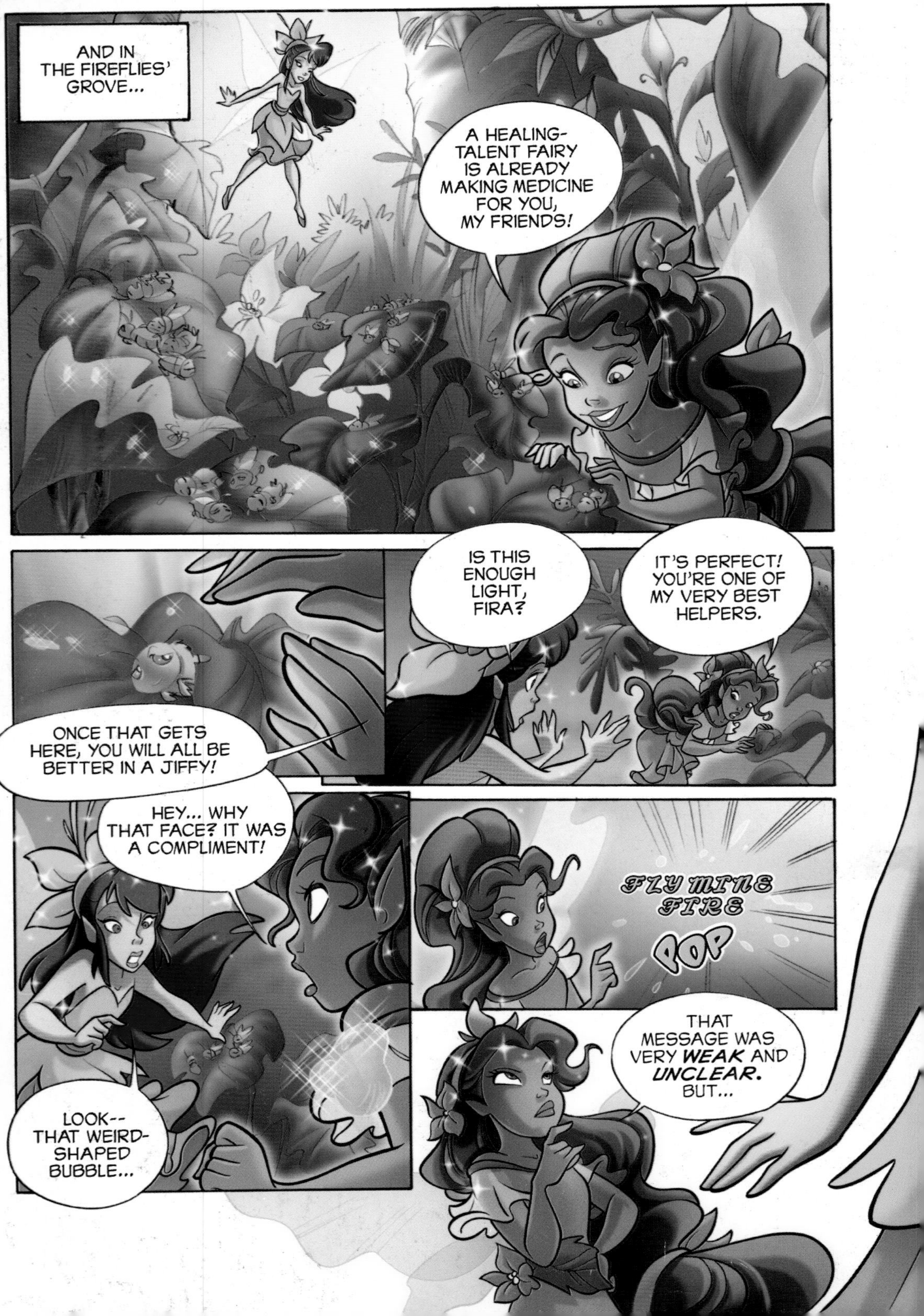
AND IN THE FIREFLIES' GROVE...
A HEALING-TALENT FAIRY IS ALREADY MAKING MEDICINE FOR YOU, MY FRIENDS!
ONCE THAT GETS HERE, YOU WILL ALL BE BETTER IN A JIFFY!
IS THIS ENOUGH LIGHT, FIRA?
IT'S PERFECT! YOU'RE ONE OF MY VERY BEST HELPERS.
HEY... WHY THAT FACE? IT WAS A COMPLIMENT!
LOOK-- THAT WEIRD-SHAPED BUBBLE...
FLY MINE FIRE
POP
THAT MESSAGE WAS VERY WEAK AND UNCLEAR. BUT...

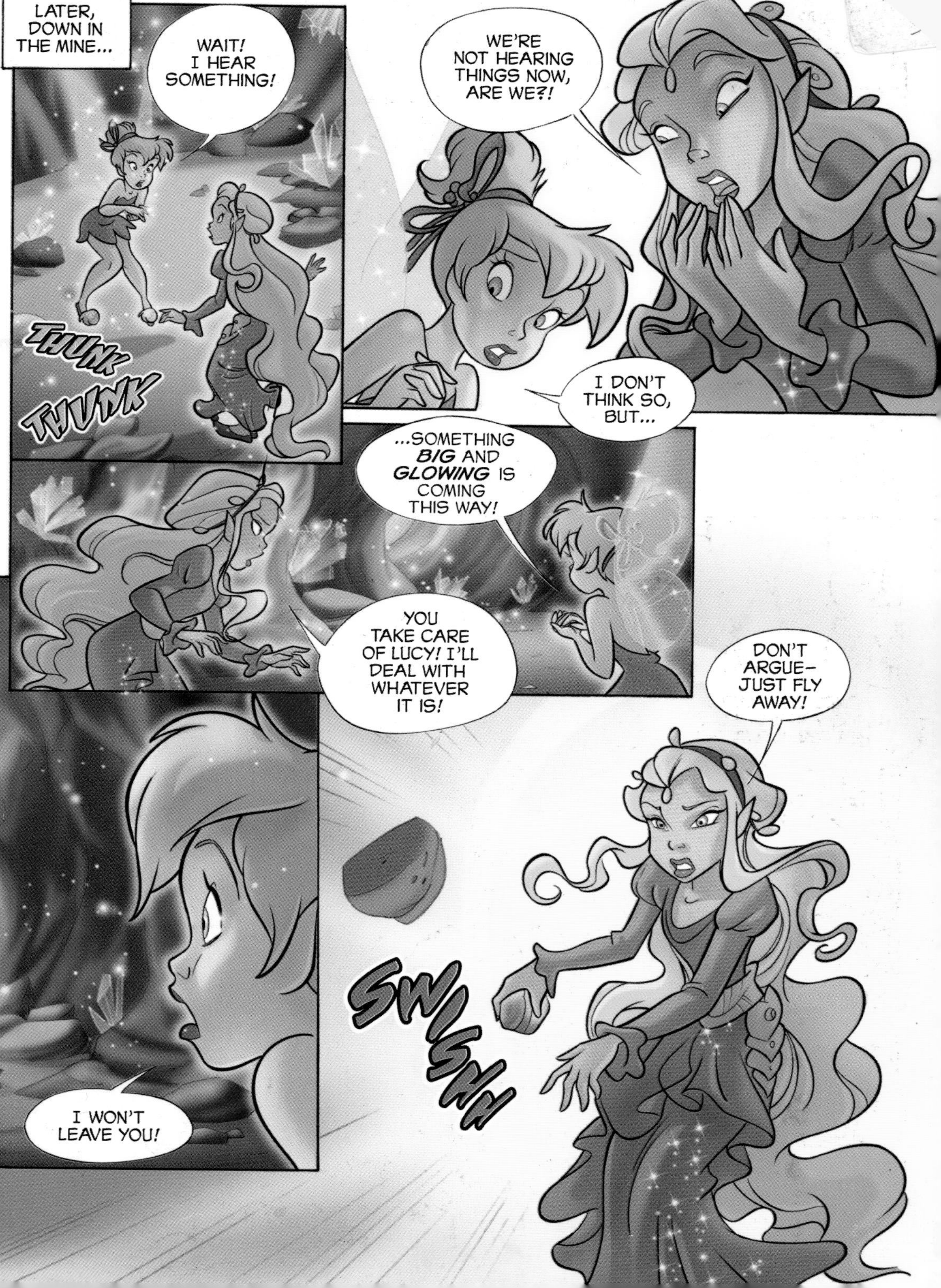
LATER, DOWN IN THE MINE...
WAIT! I HEAR SOMETHING!
THUNK
THUNK
WE'RE NOT HEARING THINGS NOW, ARE WE?!
I DON'T THINK SO, BUT...
...SOMETHING BIG AND GLOWING IS COMING THIS WAY!
YOU TAKE CARE OF LUCY! I'LL DEAL WITH WHATEVER IT IS!
DON'T ARGUE– JUST FLY AWAY!
I WON'T LEAVE YOU!
SWISHH

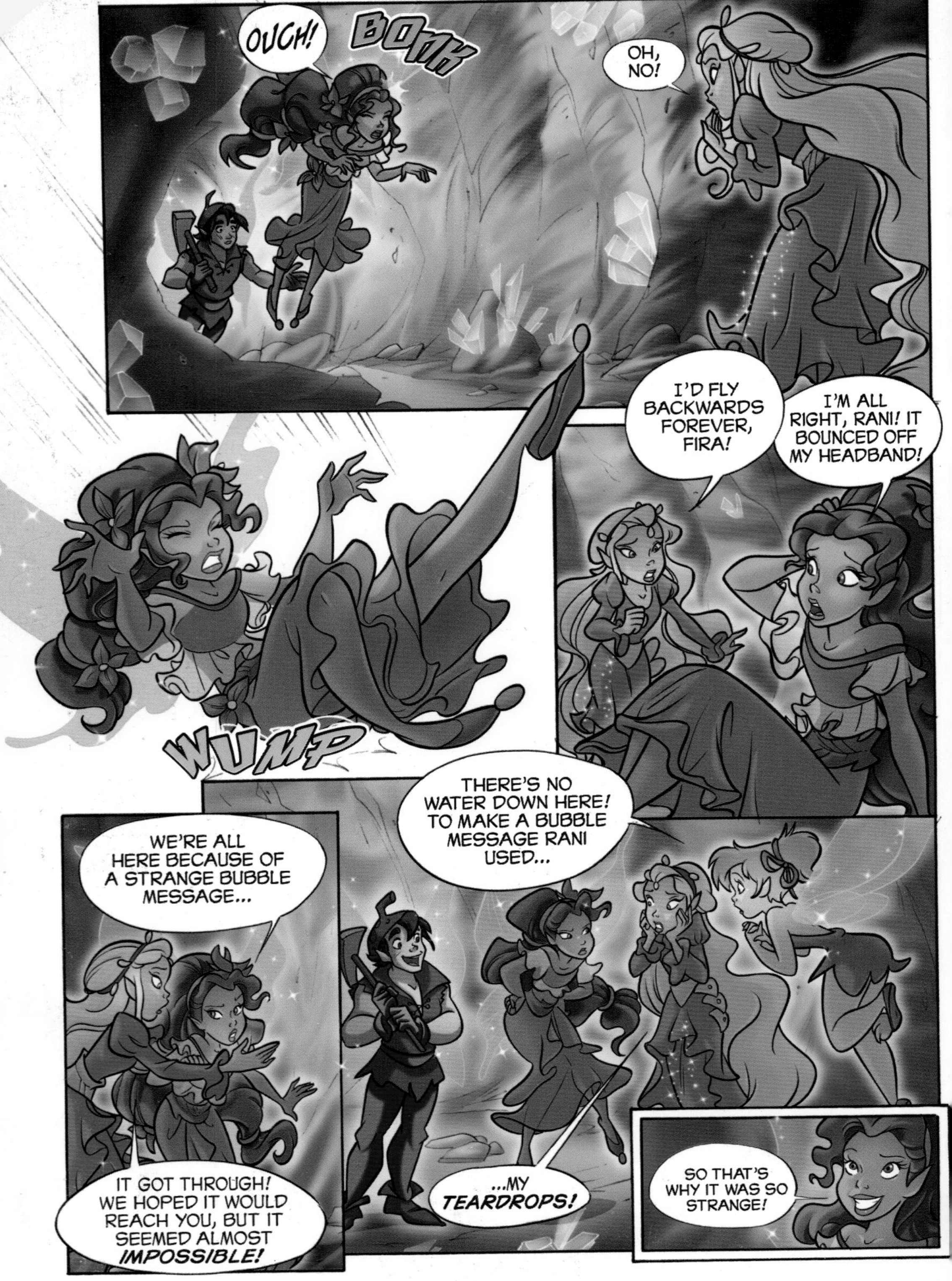
OUCH!
BONK
OH, NO!
WUMP
I'D FLY BACKWARDS FOREVER, FIRA!
I'M ALL RIGHT, RANI! IT BOUNCED OFF MY HEADBAND!
WE'RE ALL HERE BECAUSE OF A STRANGE BUBBLE MESSAGE...
IT GOT THROUGH! WE HOPED IT WOULD REACH YOU, BUT IT SEEMED ALMOST *IMPOSSIBLE!*
THERE'S NO WATER DOWN HERE! TO MAKE A BUBBLE MESSAGE RANI USED...
...MY *TEARDROPS!*
SO THAT'S WHY IT WAS SO STRANGE!

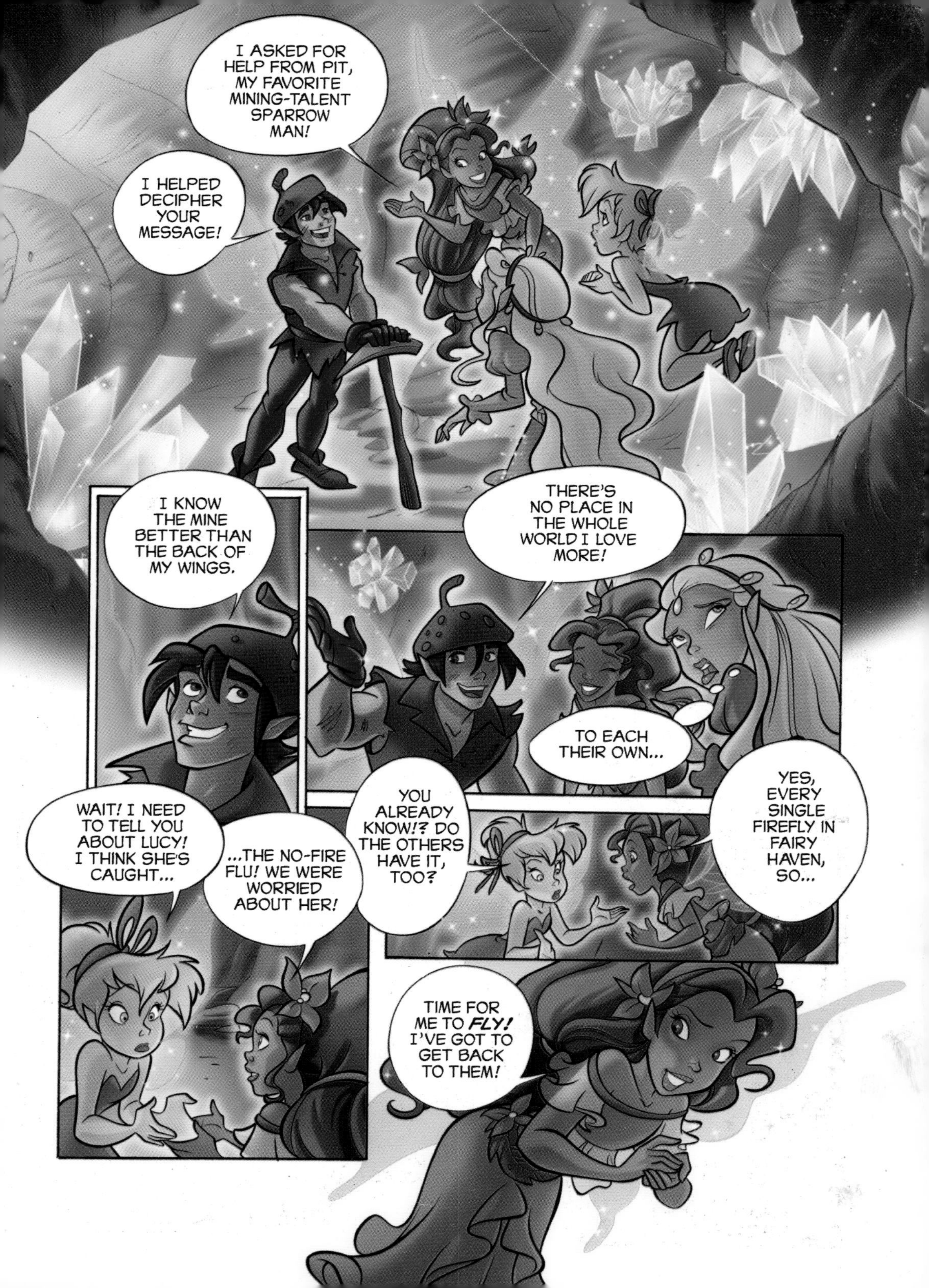

I ASKED FOR HELP FROM PIT, MY FAVORITE MINING-TALENT SPARROW MAN!
I HELPED DECIPHER YOUR MESSAGE!
I KNOW THE MINE BETTER THAN THE BACK OF MY WINGS.
THERE'S NO PLACE IN THE WHOLE WORLD I LOVE MORE!
TO EACH THEIR OWN...
WAIT! I NEED TO TELL YOU ABOUT LUCY! I THINK SHE'S CAUGHT...
...THE NO-FIRE FLU! WE WERE WORRIED ABOUT HER!
YOU ALREADY KNOW!? DO THE OTHERS HAVE IT, TOO?
YES, EVERY SINGLE FIREFLY IN FAIRY HAVEN, SO...
TIME FOR ME TO FLY! I'VE GOT TO GET BACK TO THEM!

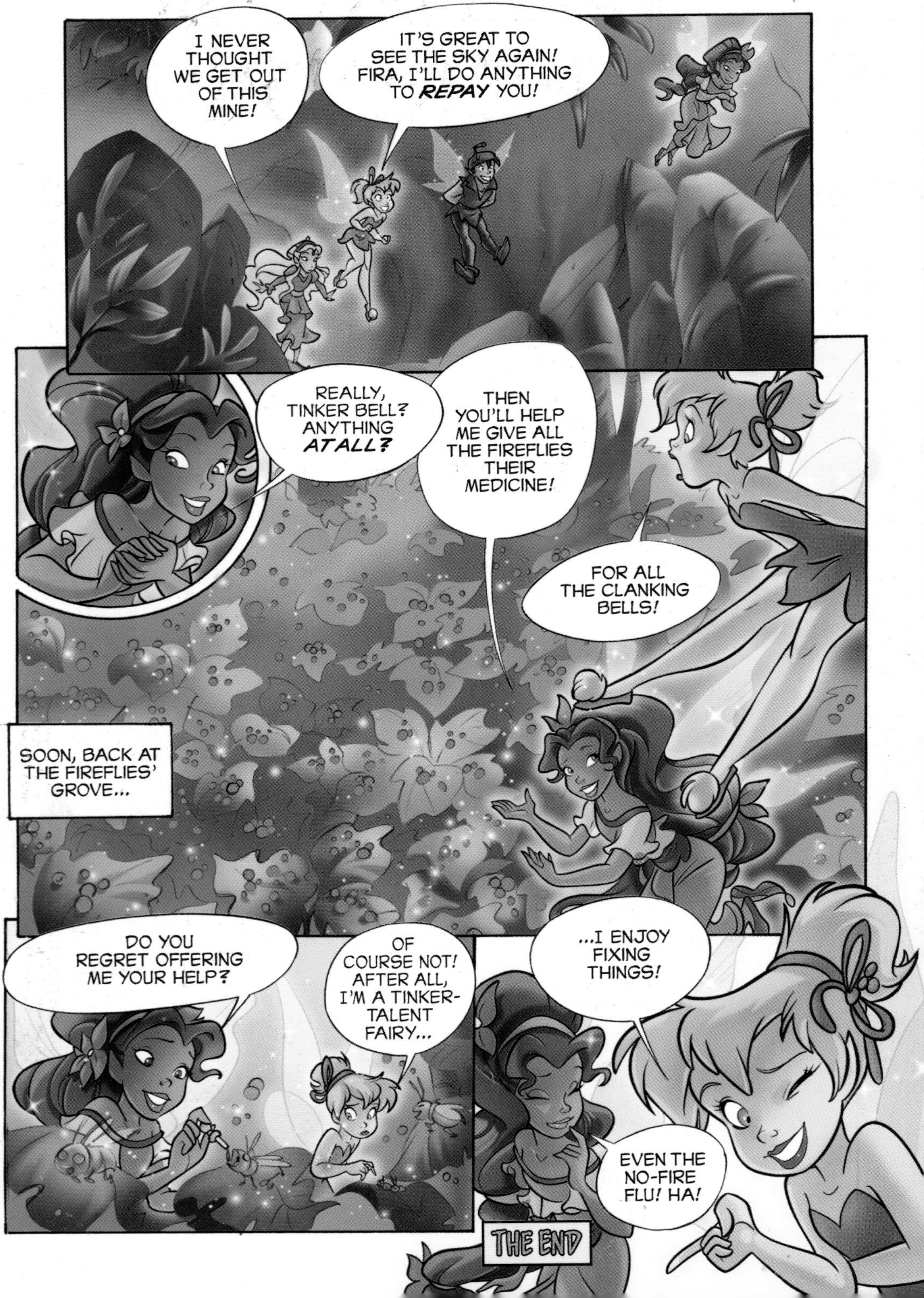
I NEVER THOUGHT WE GET OUT OF THIS MINE!
IT'S GREAT TO SEE THE SKY AGAIN! FIRA, I'LL DO ANYTHING TO REPAY YOU!
REALLY, TINKER BELL? ANYTHING AT ALL?
THEN YOU'LL HELP ME GIVE ALL THE FIREFLIES THEIR MEDICINE!
FOR ALL THE CLANKING BELLS!
SOON, BACK AT THE FIREFLIES' GROVE...
DO YOU REGRET OFFERING ME YOUR HELP?
OF COURSE NOT! AFTER ALL, I'M A TINKER-TALENT FAIRY...
...I ENJOY FIXING THINGS!
EVEN THE NO-FIRE FLU! HA!
THE END

WATCH OUT FOR

PAPERCUTZ ™

Welcome to the fifth fantabulous DISNEY FAIRIES graphic novel from Papercutz. I'm Jim Salicrup, your pixilated Papercutz Editor-in-Chief, and have I got BIG news! If you've already picked up the first four DISNEY FAIRIES graphic novels then you've no doubt already noticed that this fifth volume is much BIGGER! Each and every page is now big enough that no one should have any problem trying to read the tiny lettering in the word balloons! And now you can really see the beautiful artwork better than ever! We're super-excited about the change and hope you are too! As always you can tell me exactly what you think by either sending me an email (Salicrup@papercutz.com) or a card or letter (Jim Salicrup, PAPERCUTZ, 40 Exchange Place, Suite 1308, New York, NY 10005).

In DISNEY FAIRIES #4 "Tinker Bell to the Rescue," Captain Hook, the big bad pirate we all love to hate, made his Papercutz graphic novel debut. And now, he's back again (see page 18) in "The Pirates Go Bananas"! With those pesky pirates appearing in our pages, the obvious question is—where's Peter Pan? Let us know if you want to see Peter in an upcoming DISNEY FAIRIES graphic novel. You know how to reach us!

And speaking of pirates, they seem to be popping up in lots of other Papercutz graphic novels as well! They're worse than bed bugs! Perhaps one of the greatest pirate stories of all time is *Treasure Island* by Robert Louis Stevenson. Some say it was Stevenson who invented just about every defining characteristic of the pirates we see in pop culture to this very day. Writer David Chauvel and artist Fred Simon faithfully adapted Stevenson's novel into comics form, and the final result is simply breathtaking! See for yourself by picking up a copy of CLASSICS ILLUSTRATED DELUXE #5 "Treasure Island"—available from booksellers everywhere. For more information about the pirates lurking about the pages of Papercutz, check out the article on the following pages.

FULL-COLOR GRAPHIC NOVEL ADAPTATION

CLASSICS Illustrated® Deluxe

TREASURE ISLAND

By Robert Louis Stevenson Adapted by Chauvel and Simon

PAPERCUTZ

But don't let all this talk about pirates upset you. Sure, they're pretty scary—but we have something that will always keep us safe—"Faith, Trust, and Pixie Dust!"

Thanks,

Jim

Who doesn't love pirates? You know, the fictional kind that say "Yaarr" and "Shiver me timbers" all the time. Papercutz Associate Editor Michael Petranek recalls that when he was a kid, he'd pick up a stick, pretend it was his sword, and join his friends aboard an abandoned 10-foot boat that they discovered in an alley in Dallas, Texas. "We weren't just playing pirates," Michael says, "we were pirates!" With the success of the Pirates of the Caribbean, featuring Johnny Depp's Captain Jack Sparrow, there seems to be no end in sight to our fascination with these nautical nasties. We thought it might be fun to take a look at the pirates that have made their way from their poopdecks and onto the pages of your favorite graphic novels. So, avast ye swabs, and gather about to hear the hoary tale of…

THE PIRATES OF PAPERCUTZ™

Much of what we think of as pirates today all began in Robert Louis Stevenson's immensely popular 1882 novel "Treasure Island," which is faithfully adapted into comics by David Chauvel and Fred Simon in CLASSICS ILLUSTRATED DELUXE #5. The story is about young Jim Hawkins and his adventures after he encounters legendary pirate Long John Silver. All the elements are here—there's a mutiny, a hunt for buried treasure, and much, much more. Here's just a brief taste of what to expect—after Long John Silver arrives on the island where they expect to find buried treasure, he betrays Dr. Livesey who helped bring him to the island. Under a white flag, Silver enters the stockade Livesey and his men are holed up at, to offer a dubious truce. Negotiations don't go well, and as seemingly diplomatic Long John Silver leaves, he reveals a bit of his true colors…

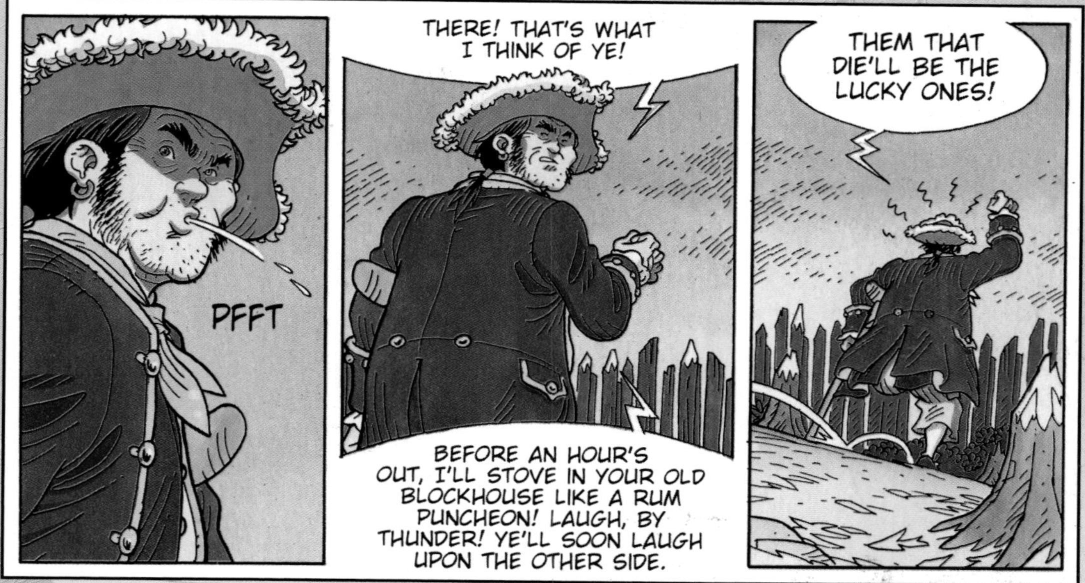

PFFT
THERE! THAT'S WHAT I THINK OF YE!
BEFORE AN HOUR'S OUT, I'LL STOVE IN YOUR OLD BLOCKHOUSE LIKE A RUM PUNCHEON! LAUGH, BY THUNDER! YE'LL SOON LAUGH UPON THE OTHER SIDE.
THEM THAT DIE'LL BE THE LUCKY ONES!

CLASSICS ILLUSTRATED DELUXE #5 "Treasure Island" not only tells an epic adventure story with dramatic battles and nail-biting moments of suspense, it also established much of what is considered pirate lore today. A few examples…

The Black Spot: A message of impending doom given from one pirate to another.

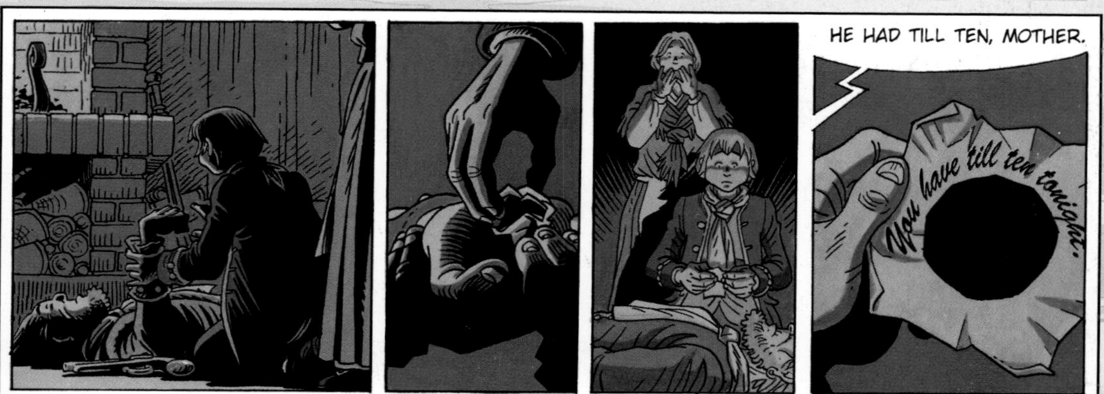

HE HAD TILL TEN, MOTHER.
You have till ten tonight.

Parrots on the Shoulders of Pirates:
Long John Silver named his parrot "Captain Flint."

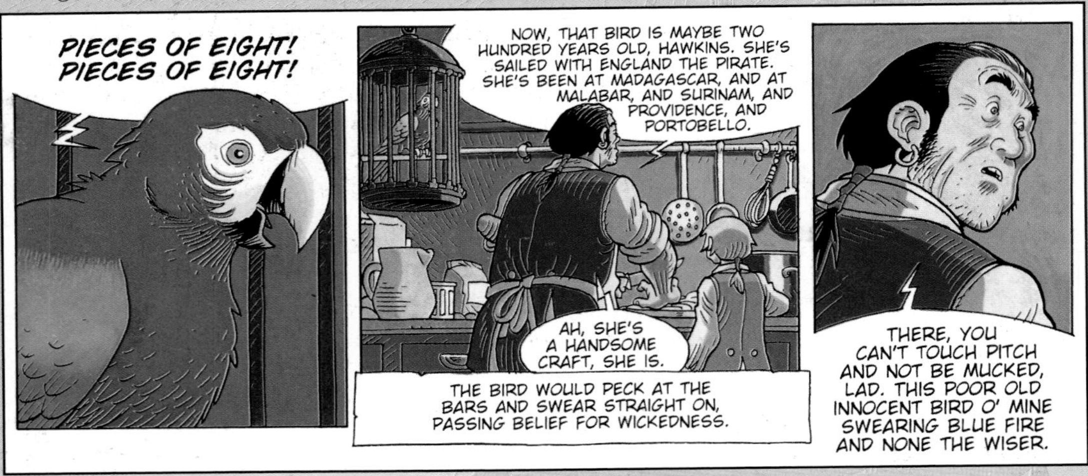
PIECES OF EIGHT! PIECES OF EIGHT!
NOW, THAT BIRD IS MAYBE TWO HUNDRED YEARS OLD, HAWKINS. SHE'S SAILED WITH ENGLAND THE PIRATE. SHE'S BEEN AT MADAGASCAR, AND AT MALABAR, AND SURINAM, AND PROVIDENCE, AND PORTOBELLO.
AH, SHE'S A HANDSOME CRAFT, SHE IS.
THE BIRD WOULD PECK AT THE BARS AND SWEAR STRAIGHT ON, PASSING BELIEF FOR WICKEDNESS.
THERE, YOU CAN'T TOUCH PITCH AND NOT BE MUCKED, LAD. THIS POOR OLD INNOCENT BIRD O' MINE SWEARING BLUE FIRE AND NONE THE WISER.

X Marks the Spot:
The dark origins of the phrase "X marks the spot" come from the British navy. When they put someone in front of a firing squad, a piece of paper with an X on it was placed upon the person who was to be executed, to provide soldiers a clear target. Treasure maps in comics and movies almost always have an "X" that marks the spot where treasure has been buried. This appears in "Treasure Island" in the form of a map that Dr. Livesey finds...

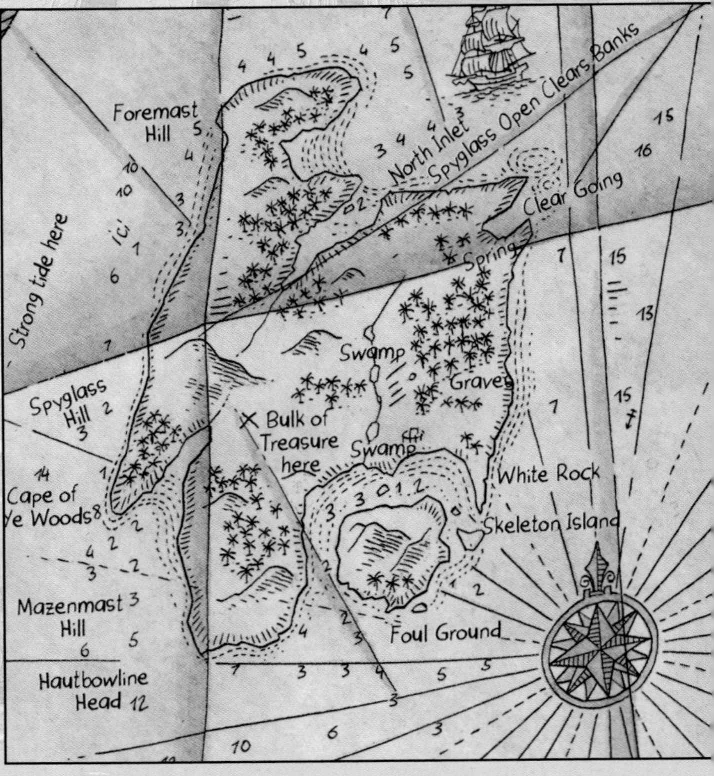
Foremast Hill
Strong tide here
North Inlet
Spyglass Open Clears Banks
Clear Going
Spring
Swamp
Graves
Spyglass Hill
X Bulk of Treasure here
Swamp
White Rock
Cape of Ye Woods
Skeleton Island
Mazenmast Hill
Foul Ground
Hautbowline Head

Robert Louis Stevenson's pirates in "Treasure Island" became the model for virtually all fictional pirates to follow. J.M. Barrie's 1904 fantasy-filled play "Peter Pan, or The Boy Who Wouldn't Grow Up" contributed Captain Hook, a pirate who "was Blackbeard's boatswain, and... the only man Long John Silver ever feared" to the pantheon of pernicious pirates. Yet, Hook's right hand was cut off by Peter Pan and swallowed by a crocodile, which is why Hook seeks revenge on Peter. Tinker Bell, Peter's feisty fairy friend was also introduced in that play, which soon became a novel, and was the inspiration for the classic Disney animated film, Peter Pan.

The DISNEY FAIRIES graphic novels have mainly focused on the adventures of Tinker Bell, and her fellow fairies Prilla, Beck, Rani, and Vidia, among others, in Pixie Hollow in Never Land. Captain Hook makes his long-awaited comics appearance in DISNEY FAIRIES graphic novel #4 "Tinker Bell to the Rescue":

In his DISNEY FAIRIES appearances, Captain Hook may not be as fearsome as Long John Silver, but he still has a lot in common with Silver. Most obviously, he is also missing a limb! The biggest difference is that Silver's adventures are more or less set in the real world, while Hook literally resides in Never Land. And do you know how to get to Never Land? It's easy! You just head toward the second star on your right and fly straight on till morning, and you'll come to Never Land. It's the flying part that's a little tricky.

Just as exciting and exotic as Treasure Island and Never Land is New Mouse City, which, as we're sure you already

NEW STORIES! FULL-COLOR GRAPHIC NOVEL
Disney fairies
TinkerBell
to the Rescue
PAPERCUT

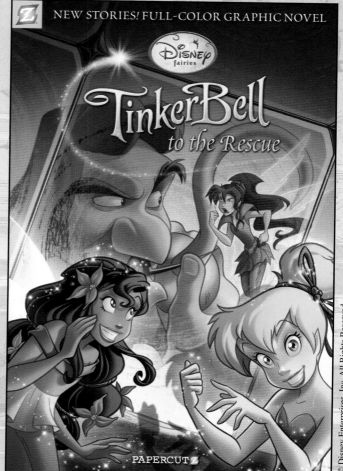

know is where Geronimo Stilton lives. Geronimo is the famouse editor of The Rodent's Gazette, and quite an adventurer himself. When not editing the great mousetropolitan newspaper, Geronimo is travelling through time to prevent the meddlesome Pirate Cats from changing history. Yes, Pirate Cats. Catardone III of Catatonia is the ruler of the Pirate Cats, and his dream is to become the richest and most famouse cat of all time. His daughter, Tersilla of Catatonia, may be the real brains behind the Pirate Cats. And Bonzo Felix is Catardone's assistant. Take a look at Bonzo and Felix as seen in GERONIMO STILTON graphic novel #6 "Who Stole the Mona Lisa?" Notice anything in particular?

HMM... SURE! WE HAVE TO KIDNAP LEONARDO DA VINCI AND BRING HIM WITH US TO CATBURG!
EXACTLY! ACCORDING TO TERSILLA, HE'S THE ONLY ONE WHO CAN DECODE THE MYSTERIOUS PARCHMENT!

While both cats share Long John Silver's fashion sense, Catardone also has a hook, instead of a hand—or is that a paw? Aside from being cats that walk upright and speak, these Pirate Cats can also travel through time in their catjet. While neither Long John Silver nor Captain Hook have ever been particularly successful, the Pirate Cats are even more incompetent. These pirates would much rather get their paws on a plate of fresh fish than a treasure chest. Yet, it would be a big mistake to think that they're pushovers. They always manage to get away to fight another day. After all, like most cats, they're always able to land on their feet.

Whether in the pages of CLASSICS ILLUSTRATED DELUXE, DISNEY FAIRIES, or GERONIMO STILTON, one thing is certain, we haven't seen the last of the pirates of Papercutz! Yaarr!